Same Love

Same Love

TONY CORREIA

JAMES LORIMER & COMPANY LTD., PUBLISHERS
TORONTO

James Lorimer & Company Ltd., Publishers acknowledges the support of
the Ontario Arts Council (OAC), an agency of the Government of Ontario,
which in 2015-16 funded 1,676 individual artists and 1,125 organizations in
209 communities across Ontario for a total of $50.5 million. We acknowledge
the support of the Canada Council for the Arts, which last year invested $153
million to bring the arts to Canadians throughout the country. This project has
been made possible in part by the Government of Canada and with the support of the Ontario Media Development Corporation.

Cover design: Shabnam Safari
Cover image: iStock

978-1-4594-1234-7
eBook also available 978-1-4594-1213-2

Cataloguing data available from Library and Archives Canada.

Published by:
James Lorimer & Company Ltd.,
Publishers
117 Peter Street, Suite 304
Toronto, ON, Canada
M5V 0M3
www.lorimer.ca

Distributed by:
Lerner Publisher Services
1251 Washington Ave N
Minneapolis, MN, USA
55401
www.lernerbooks.com

Printed and bound in Canada.
Manufactured by Friesens Corporation in Altona, Manitoba, Canada in
January 2017.
Job #229624

In loving memory of Aaron Hachey,
secret handshake buddy.

Fall into the Gap

MIKE'S EYES ARE WIDE AS SAUCERS as he watches me end the call with my mother. I tuck my phone back into my pocket.

"Did she believe you?" he asks.

"I think so."

"I can't believe we're finally hanging out!" He claps his hands like a contestant on a game show.

"Sorry for all the sneaking around," I tell him. "It's easier to lie."

"I'm glad you decided to be yourself for a couple of hours — even if it means shopping at Metrotown Mall."

"I'm so embarrassed to have to lie. I mean, you're a friend from school."

"Don't worry, I get it. You're closeted, white, and Christian. I'm fierce, brown, and gay. We're Romeo and Juliet without the heaving bosoms."

"Which one of us is Juliet?"

"Girl, you are definitely the Juliet in this movie. Like Romeo, I will cut a bitch before I let anyone tell me who I can and can't love."

"Stop calling me girl. No one can know I'm gay until I graduate."

"Closet case," he shoots at me.

"Drag queen," I shoot back.

"It's not an insult if it's true, honey. Now where do you want to go? Abercrombie & Fitch? We can judge all the posers."

"I can't — too much perfume. My parents will smell it on my clothes."

"Are you telling me you're not allowed to go into A&F?"

"A&F is the gay bar of the shopping mall as far as Christians are concerned."

"How about The Gap? Is that a gateway to hell in your religion?"

"I like The Gap."

"You would. Onward homo," Mike says. He leads the charge down the mall.

I can barely keep up as he makes his way through the crowd of shoppers, dodging duck-faced girls posing for selfies, mothers dragging their children and their husbands — who are pretending not look at the duck-faced girls. I keep looking around in case someone from my church sees Mike and me together.

"They should change the name of this store to Fifty Shades of Beige," Mike says. He frowns as he sifts through the rack.

"Do you want to go someplace else?" I ask.

"This is fine. Do your thing."

"I feel like I'm disappointing you."

"It's not you, Adam, it's the clothes. When I look around this store it makes me think that everyone is trying to look like each other — even the brown people. It's so boring."

"That reminds me, I've been working on this really cool graphic novel. It's about a preacher who uses an app to brainwash his followers into believing God is speaking to them on their phones."

"Sounds cool. When do I get to read it?"

"I just started it. I can only work on it after my parents go to bed and on my breaks at work."

"Why don't you just tell your parents you're gay?" Mike asks.

"Not until next year, once I've been accepted to university," I tell him. "I've saved every penny I've ever earned so I can study to become a graphic artist. But it's still not enough. If my parents don't help me out, I'll have to take out a ton of student loans and be in debt for the rest of my life."

"Word!" Mike raises his hand to Jesus. "Ain't nobody got time for that."

"Does it bother you that we have to keep our friendship secret?"

"It's a drag — and not in a good way! But I understand. You're not the first person I've met with religious parents. Wait till you meet some of the people at the gay youth group downtown. They'll blow your mind."

"I hate all this sneaking around," I tell him. "I hate that I have to memorize your number and delete all your texts in case my parents snoop through my phone. I honestly don't know why you want to be friends with me when there are so many rules."

"Because you're a good guy, Adam," Mike says. "And an amazing artist. Some of the illustrations you did for the yearbook blew me away. I can't wait until you're rich and famous so I can tell people I knew you when you were a scared little boy."

"Stop it."

"I'm serious. But you need to stop being so hard on yourself. All of this fabulousness did not happen overnight," Mike waves his hands over his body.

"Trust me, my dad was not thrilled to have Beyonce for a son."

"It won't be like this forever, I promise."

Mike holds a plaid shirt up to his chest and says, "Does this shirt make my ass look fat?"

"No, but flannel makes you look like a lesbian."

"Don't joke about lesbians," Mike says. "I learned that lesson the hard way in the Gay–Straight Alliance."

Suddenly I hear the last voice in the world I want to hear. It's like the Wicked Witch from *The Wizard of Oz*.

"Adam Lethbridge, is that you?"

I turn around, and there is Mom's best friend.

"Mrs. Harris!" I give her a fake hug.

Greta Harris is one of those phony Christians who spread the word of God to your face and gossip behind your back. She's Christianity's answer to TMZ. Just when I think my luck can't get any worse, Greta's daughter Michelle appears next to her.

"Hi, Adam," she smiles.

Gross. Michelle Harris has been trying to get

inside my pants since kindergarten. Beneath that good Christian girl act beats the heart of a hussy.

"Hey, Michelle," Mike says.

"Mike Hoskins? What are you two doing here together?" asks Michelle. She is looking at us like she caught us making out.

"I'm sorry, who did you say your friend was again?" Greta asks. There's a twinkle in her eye, like a reporter sniffing out a scoop.

"Oh, we're not friends." Then I realize how awful that just sounded. I start speaking faster, trying to cover my tracks. "Mike and I worked on the yearbook together. I was on my way home from work and we happened to run into each other."

"Two boys shopping for clothes," Greta says. "How interesting."

"Tell me about it," says Michelle.

I wish they would both just fly away on the broom they came in on.

"Look at the time!" Greta glances at an invisible wristwatch. "We should get going if we're going to beat the traffic. Say hello to your mother for me, Adam."

And just like that, Greta disappears into the crowd like it was a cloud of black smoke.

"You didn't tell me you're friends with Michelle Harris!" Mike says. "I hate that bitch! She's always ranting about religious freedom. She claims she's discriminated against because of her faith. Oh, Adam, are you okay? You look like you're going to throw up."

"Don't take this wrong way but . . . you know how you're kind of flamboyant?"

"That's putting it mildly, if I say so myself."

"You see, Greta has a really big mouth. She's probably on her phone right now with my mother telling her she saw us together."

"She wouldn't!"

"She would, and she would enjoy it."

"You're overreacting."

"Where do you think Michelle gets it from?"

"Are you telling me your parents are as religious as Michelle? No wonder you've been sneaking around behind their backs."

"Exactly. I should go home."

"Is there anything I can do to help?" Mike asks.

"Can you turn back time?"

"Girl, I may be fierce, but I'm not Cher."

02 Secret Sketchbook

I'M DRIPPING WITH SWEAT by the time I get home. I try to compose myself before I open the front door. If I act natural, I might be able to defuse the situation.

"Adam, is that you?" Mom calls from the kitchen.

Would a burglar use a key to get in? My parents have no idea how funny I am. No one does, except Mike.

"Hi, Mom!"

"Can you come to the kitchen please?"

Mom and Dad are seated at the kitchen table. Their faces are like stone.

"Did someone die?" I ask.

"In a sense," Mom says. Mom is in her early forties, but looks older.

"Give me your phone," Dad says, holding out his hand.

"What for?" I can barely look at them; I'm so ashamed of myself right now.

"I said give me your phone," he repeats.

I hand it over. He unlocks it and starts swiping his finger across the screen. He's not going to find anything. I deleted all the texts from Mike as well as my call log as I rode the SkyTrain home.

"We got a call from Greta Harris a while ago. She said that she and Michelle saw you with a faggot from school," Mom says.

"Mike? We bumped into each other at the mall. I was being polite," I say. I feel bad for betraying Mike by lying. "According to Greta the two of you looked like you were having a gay old time shopping for new outfits," Dad says. He swishes around the kitchen doing a bad imitation of a girl.

"Lawrence, stop it." Mom has the decency to look embarrassed by my dad's behaviour.

"Did Greta really say that about me?" I ask.

"She said she saw you on a date with the gayest kid at your school," Mom says.

"We were only talking," I protest.

"Did you or did you not call me two hours ago to say your manager asked you to cover for someone at work?"

Oops! "They found someone else to cover the shift. What's the big deal?"

"You lied to your mother so you could go on a date with your faggot friend!" Dad yells.

I tense up like an explosion has just gone off. I'm so sick of being afraid. "We weren't on a *date*!" I insist.

"Then why did we find *this* in your room?" Dad opens a cupboard and pulls out a sketchbook. It's the secret sketchbook I've been using for one of my graphic novels.

"You went through my room?"

"It's our house, Adam. You just live here," Mom says.

"What is this filth?" Dad points at a page. "There are drawings of boys kissing boys in here!"

"It's not mine!" I lie. "I'm keeping it for a friend."

"Your name is all over this book!" Dad shouts.

"Stop it! Both of you!" Mom breaks in. "Adam, will you please tell us what is going on? What does this book have to do with that boy Greta saw you with?"

"Mike and I worked on the yearbook last year," I try to stick as close to the truth as possible.

"Then how do you explain the drawings in this book?" Mom asks.

I want to tell them that sketchbook is the only thing that's kept me sane these last eight months. I've been trying to write a graphic novel about how our church tries to fit you into a certain mould, and if you deviate from it they crush your spirit. The heroes of the story are a pair of teenagers who fall in love. I was going to toss it out because I was afraid of getting caught, but I couldn't. There were some really good sketches I thought I could use to apply to university.

"It's just a comic book," I mumble.

"Comics?" Dad says. "Your idea of comics is pictures of boys kissing! Those aren't comics. That's sick!"

"The Bible is filled with stories, and that's what you choose to draw?" Mom asks. Her disappointment is worse than my dad's anger. "You could be the next Michelangelo if you put your mind to it."

A joke Mike told me pops into my head: *If a straight artist painted the Sistine Chapel it would be beige.* I start to laugh in spite of the situation.

"Do you think this is *funny*?" Dad fumes.

"No! Not at all!" I say.

"I'm afraid to ask this," Mom says, "But are you having sex with boys?"

"No!"

"Do you want to?" she asks.

What I want to do is run out of the house and never look back. But with my phone in my dad's clutches, there's no way I can call Mike for help. My head is spinning. I begin to wonder if I left my sketchbook out on purpose so they could find it.

"Answer your mother!" Dad says.

I want to tell my mother what she wants to hear, but I've run out of lies.

"Yes, Mom. I'm gay. I'm sorry you had to learn about it this way. I've tried to change, I swear. But I can't."

"I knew it!" Dad says, slamming his hand on the table. "You're a faggot. I knew it the day you came home crying from hockey practice. I told your mother after you went to bed. 'Marie, our boy is a faggot,' I said."

"Please stop saying that word," I say.

"What? *Faggot?*" Dad spits the word out. "That's what you are, Adam, a faggot!"

"That's enough!" It's almost a shout — the first time Mom has raised her voice to my father. We both live in fear of his temper. "Can we please deal with this like adults?"

She starts sobbing. I go to comfort her, but Dad gets in my way.

"You've done enough harm for one day," Dad says. "Go to your room and leave your laptop outside your door."

I try not to cry as I leave the kitchen and go upstairs to my room. I set my laptop in the hall and close the door behind me.

I doze off for a couple hours. The sound of Mom knocking on my door wakes me.

"Do you want to have dinner at the table or in your room?" she asks.

"I'm not really hungry," I reply. I'm actually starving. But I don't want to see my father's face right now. I can't erase the image of him prancing around the kitchen. Is that what he really thinks of me?

"I'll make you a sandwich just in case."

"Thanks."

"Your father and I called Pastor Connell for advice."

"What did he say?"

"He prayed for us — you especially."

"That was nice of him I guess."

"We made an appointment to see him after church tomorrow, okay?"

"Okay."

"Let me go make that sandwich for you."

Mom is about to close the door again. She stops like she's about to say something. For a brief second I think she's going to tell me she loves me, but something stops her. In that moment I have no idea if things with my mom will ever be the same again.

03 *Sea to Sky*

MOM AND I HAVE BEEN DRIVING for nearly an hour. I'm not allowed to speak to her when she's behind the wheel because it distracts her from the directions the GPS, suction-cupped to the windshield of the car, is giving her. Mom puts as much faith in that stupid GPS as she does in God. At least she follows its directions. Dad always second-guesses it, probably because the voice is a woman's. Dad would get lost before he'd take orders from a woman, even if it's a computer.

"Here we are!" Mom says, like we've arrived at Disneyland. She pulls into the Walmart parking lot, pointing the car towards a man standing beside a school bus. There's a large banner on the side that says "Camp Revelation."

After a two-hour session with Pastor Connell, it was decided I would be spending the next four weeks at Camp Revelation. Teens at church call it "Juvie for Christians." Registration had already closed for the summer, but Pastor Connell knows the camp organizer, Bishop Andrews, and was able to "pull a favour" for us.

My first impulse was to refuse to go. Then I pictured my father's impression of me prancing around the kitchen. That was all the convincing I needed. In a strange twist of fate, Mom and I had to go back to The Gap where Greta caught me with Mike. Turns out khakis and polo tops are the only things we're allowed to wear at the camp.

"I guess this is goodbye," I say. I grab my duffel bag from the back seat, and open the car door.

"Wait," Mom says, digging through her purse. She hands me my phone and five twenty-dollar bills, as well as a brand new sketchbook and some pencils. "Don't tell your father."

"I won't. I promise. Thanks, Mom."

I move in to give her a kiss, but she turns her head and my lips bash into her ear. It's the first time she's ever refused a kiss from me.

"I should go," I say. I shove my phone and the money into my pockets. "I'll see you in a month."

"I'll pray for you," she says.

I'm barely out of the car when she turns on the ignition and drives away.

I throw my duffel bag over my shoulder and walk towards the school bus. Faces stare out the windows as I approach the door. Everyone avoids eye contact with me. When I get closer I realize the man by the bus is not much older than me, twenty years old at the most.

"I'm Brian. You must be Adam," He yanks my arm as he shakes my hand. "We've been waiting for you."

Brian is dressed in khakis and a red polo shirt with a gold cross embroidered above his heart. His hair is parted perfectly to one side and his cheeks are plump and smooth like a baby's. He has the face of someone who has never known disappointment his whole life.

"Sorry I'm late. My mom is an overly cautious driver," I tell him.

"Don't be silly. You're right on time, but you are the last of the campers to arrive." He makes it sound like I've lost points. "First we need to take care of a couple of tasks and then we'll be on our way. Please hand over your phone."

"I knew there wasn't any cell reception at the camp. I didn't realize you were taking our phones away."

"Screens get between you and God."

"Can't I keep it until we get to the camp?" I'm not married to my phone, but I just got it back. I wanted to text Mike and let him know that I'm okay.

"Trust me, you'll thank me for taking this away. Everyone does," Brian says.

I give him my phone, which he puts in a plastic Ziploc bag with my name on it.

"Do you have any books or magazines with you?" he asks me.

"I was going to read *Archie Digest* on the bus."

"I loved Archie when I was your age," Brian says. "But I'm afraid Archie is on the list of banned reading material. I'm going to have to take that too."

"You said you love Archie."

"That was before they introduced a gay character."

"Kevin Keller isn't in this issue!"

"You'll get it back at the end of the summer with your phone. By then, you probably won't even want it."

Brian throws the comic book into the bag with my phone. He pulls a bound book out of the bag hanging over his shoulder. "Here's a copy of the camp handbook. You can read that to pass the time."

"Can I keep my sketchbook at least?" I ask.

"Oh for sure. Go find a seat on the bus while I load your bag into the luggage van," Brian says.

I watch Brian drag my duffel bag to a waiting van, and then I step onto the bus. It feels like the first day of school. The bus is about half full. Most everyone has their own seat, and are either pretending to be asleep or pretending I'm invisible. I start walking down the aisle hoping someone will make room for me. I strike gold about halfway down the bus.

"Take a load off." A girl with mischievous eyes scoots over to the window seat.

"Thanks," I say as I take the aisle seat next to her. "I'm Adam."

"Rhonda. What are you in for?"

"Beg your pardon?"

"You're some kind of sinner. It's written all over your face."

"I had an abortion."

"You have a sick sense of humour. I like that."

"I'm gay," I whisper. "Can't you tell from my lisp? What are you in for?"

"My parents caught me having sex with my boyfriend."

"Brutal."

"And he's Muslim."

"Ouch."

Once Brian is on the bus, it lurches forward and out of the Walmart parking lot.

Rhonda and I flip through the Camp Revelation handbook as we drive up the Sea to Sky highway. The handbook is a centimetre-thick stack of photocopied pages filled with numbered lists and typos. The camp organizers have managed to come up with a rule for every possible sin we could commit. There are rules about the length of our hair (public, not pubic). Rules about how long we can be alone in the bathroom (15 minutes). Rules about touching other campers (handshakes are allowed but no lingering hands on shoulders). Rules about the books we can read and the music we can listen to (Christian or nothing). My favourites are the rules about our underwear (no Calvin Klein).

"It's a good thing I didn't pack my thong," I whisper to Rhonda. She cackles like a mad woman.

"I can hear you two," Brian shouts from the front of the bus. He checks his list. "Adam and Rhonda, if you don't behave I'm going to separate you."

"See how you are? You're already getting me in trouble," Rhonda says.

I open my new sketchbook on my lap. I can smell the clean white sheets of paper. The book's spine crackles a little as I flatten the cover. I take a pencil out of the pack and begin to draw a silly picture of Brian while Rhonda watches, enthralled. The tension from saying goodbye to Mom slowly slips away. So does the city, as streets and buildings give way to trees and mountains. Maybe Camp Revelation was what I needed after all.

04 Room 120

WE TURN OFF THE SEA TO SKY highway onto an old road that hugs the side of a mountain. The trees act as blinds as we pass them by, letting in sticks of light that blind us every five seconds. The hill is so steep it feels like someone is lifting the bus from the front. The higher we get, the harder it is not to imagine us going over the side of the cliff. The bus grinds its way up the gravel road, past the tree line. There's nothing but mountain peaks for miles around. I can see the Pacific

Ocean in the distance and the light reflecting off the glass skyscrapers in Vancouver.

The bus makes another turn. Now the landscape looks like the surface of a deserted planet. There are large patches of brown grass and small clumps of trees. I breathe a sigh of relief when we reach level ground again. The bus stops in front of a lodge the size of a McMansion.

"Would you get a load of that thing?" Rhonda says.

"It looks like the house in Hansel and Gretel."

"Totally."

"We're here!" Brian shouts back at us.

We shuffle off the bus like senior citizens in line at Tim Hortons. Two women and a man dressed in the camp uniform come out of the lodge to greet us.

"All right everyone," Brian shouts, clapping his hands. "Kindly gather your bags from the luggage van. The counsellors and I will give you your room assignments."

I get in line behind Rhonda. When it's my turn, I speak to another guy in his twenties holding a clipboard. He kind of looks like Brian's evil twin.

"Welcome to Camp Revelation. I'm Brad," he says. "And you are?"

"Adam Lethbridge."

"You're in room 120. Just go in and take a left down the first hall off of the common area. There's a map in your handbook if you get lost," Brad says. "Your bunkmates arrived this morning. Brian will be by in a bit to see if you need anything."

I lug my duffel bag onto my shoulder and head into the lodge. The first thing I see is a huge living room that looks like it hasn't changed since the sixties. It reminds me of a villain's secret lair in an old spy movie. This is awesome!

I walk down the hall looking for room 120. All the doors are open and I can see into people's rooms. I feel awkward, staring at the boys relaxing on their bunks as I scan the door numbers. Room 120 is at the end of the hall. There are bunk beds on each side of the room. I see two of my new roommates reading on the lower bunks. I knock gently on the door.

They lower their books and give me the once over.

"Hi. I'm Adam." I wave a meek hello.

The guy on the right side of the room sets aside his Bible and gets up from the bed.

"Nice to meet you, Adam. I'm Randall. That's Martin." He points to the shaggy-haired First Nations guy on the opposite bunk. "Paul? Aren't you going to say hello to our new friend?" Randall yells up to the top bunk.

An Asian guy sits up in his bunk. His hair is pushed to one side from lying on it.

"What now?" Paul snarls.

I can tell this guy is going to be a barrel of laughs for the summer. But his rudeness makes him sort of attractive. So do his dark eyes and the way his perfect lips curl when he snarls. *What's wrong with me?*

"Let me help you with your things," Randall says, taking my duffel bag from me. "We saved you a dresser drawer. And there's a closet near the front of the room if you need to hang anything."

All the attention from Randall is making me nervous. The look in his eyes reminds me of the creepy men who would hit on me at the bookstore where I worked.

"Are you settling in, Adam?" Brian pokes his head into our room. He doesn't give me a chance to respond before he says, "This is Randall's second year at the camp. He should be able to answer any questions. Otherwise, everything you need to know is in your handbook."

"I'm sure I can fulfill all of Adam's needs," Randall says.

Martin groans from behind a paperback copy of *Left Behind* — the Christian thriller about The Rapture.

"I expect to see all of you at the icebreaker tonight. If you need me, my room is at the end of the hall." And like that, Brian is gone.

"You have to see our view. It's incredible," Randall says. He leads me to an old desk and chair next to the open window. "Have a seat and breathe in that fresh mountain air."

"Give the guy some space, Randall," Martin says. "He just got here."

"You'll have to excuse Martin. He's already decided he hates it here," Randall explains.

"I heard that," Martin says.

"I wanted you to."

Paul breaks in. "Get a room, you two."

"Give me a break," Randall says. "I wouldn't kiss Martin for all the tea in China. Sorry, Paul. That was racist."

"I'm Korean, so no offence taken," Paul says.

"Well don't just stand there," Randall says, turning to me. "Have a seat."

I lower my butt into the chair and make myself comfortable. Randall is right. The view is amazing. My fingers are itching to get it down in my sketchbook.

"You got him to sit in the chair. Are you happy now, Randall?" Martin asks.

"I'm just being friendly," Randall snaps back.

"You're being a stalker," Martin says.

"Are you guys going to act like this the entire

month?" Paul asks. I can tell he's already tired of it. "This is supposed to be a retreat."

"Martin started it," Randall says under his breath as he goes back to his bed to sulk.

I stay seated in the chair even though I really need to pee. I'm afraid that if I get up, it's going to start another argument between Martin and Randall. I close my eyes and try to take my mind off my bladder. And then it hits me. I've only been here for ten minutes, and I already feel like I don't belong here.

05 The Icebreaker

RANDALL WILL NOT SHUT UP about the stupid icebreaker. It's all he talks about through dinner and after we get back to our room. I can see why he gets on Martin's nerves.

"I don't know why you're so excited," Martin says to Randall. "It's not like there's going to be any booze."

"You don't need booze to have fun at a party," Randall says.

"Have you ever been to a party?" Martin asks him.

"Our church has a social every month," Randall says proudly.

"Give me a break," Martin huffs. "Even Jesus drank wine at the Last Supper."

"That's not funny," Randall says.

"Actually it was a little funny," Paul says. Was that the hint of a smile?

"I expected more from you, Paul," Randall says.

"Based on what?" Paul asks.

Time for a change of subject. "What should I wear?" I ask as I go through my clothes. "A polo top and khakis? Or a polo top and khakis?"

"Take a risk. How about a polo top and khakis?" Paul suggests.

Hmm. This Paul guy knows how to pick up and carry a joke. He's more than a pretty face.

"If you three are going to be like this for the rest of the summer I'm going to ask to be moved into another room," Randall complains.

"Promise?" says Martin hopefully.

Randall closes his eyes and tries to pull himself together. Something tells me he enjoys being teased more than he lets on. It's probably the most attention he's had in months.

The icebreaker is being held in the mess hall where we ate dinner. The tables have been moved aside and the walls decorated with balloons and streamers. A refreshment table is set up. Christian pop music is playing on an mp3 player that's plugged into some speakers.

"And I thought high school dances were tragic," someone says in my ear. I turn around and see Rhonda. She's standing next to a plain-looking girl with straight blonde hair.

"How's it going?" I ask, wondering if I look as gay as I feel when I give her a hug. "Guys, this is Rhonda. We met on the bus. Rhonda, these are my roommates Paul, Martin, and Randall."

"Nice to meet you," Rhonda says. "This is my roommate Sarah, who has already called me a slut because I'm not a virgin."

"I didn't call you a slut," says Sarah, rolling her eyes. "I implied it. I'm going to talk to Martha."

Rhonda watches Sarah walk away. "I'm so going to turn her into a lesbian before the summer is over."

"You're a lesbian?" Randall asks her.

"No. I'm a slut, remember?"

"We are totally hanging out this summer," Martin says to Rhonda.

"So, Adam, what do you think so far?" Rhonda asks.

"I'm loving this lodge," I reply. "It's like something out of the Gold Rush."

"It's cool isn't it?" says Paul.

"It's probably First Nations land," Martin says.

"Don't be silly," Randall says. "It was meant to be a ski resort in the sixties but the developer ran out of money. You can still see the cement pilings for the ski lift on the side of the mountain."

"I have to admit the view takes my mind off the fact that I'm here," Rhonda says.

I'm just about to agree when a voice comes over the speakers. "Can I have your attention please?"

We all look in the direction of the refreshments table, where a man with a comb-over is standing with a mic. He is by far the oldest person I have seen since I got here. Something about him disturbs me. Is it that his polo top doesn't quite cover his belly? Or that his smile doesn't seem real, like he practises it in the mirror?

"I'm Bishop Andrews, the founder of Camp Revelation," he announces. "I want to welcome everyone to another summer at Camp Revelation. For those of you who are returning: welcome back. For the newcomers: welcome to the flock. I would like to introduce you all to your camp counsellors. Please give a big round of applause for Brian, Brad, Tania, and Becky."

The four counsellors jog to form a line next to Bishop and wave to us.

"So Brian and Brad aren't the same person," I say.

When Paul giggles a little, it warms my heart.

Randall shushes us with a frown.

"Before we begin your best summer ever, I would like to say a little prayer," Bishop says. We bow our heads as Bishop asks God to bless us with a fun and safe summer filled with His love. As soon as Bishop says, "Amen," the icebreaker turns into a party again.

I have a better time at the icebreaker than I thought I would. I ended up meeting a ton of people. I just assumed that the other campers would be uptight Christians like Greta and Michelle Harris. There are a few of those, but for the most part everyone seems okay.

"All right, everybody," Brian says into the microphone. "Time for karaoke!"

"Who wants to do a duet with me?" Paul says. Randall, Martin, and Rhonda all take a giant step back, leaving me alone next to Paul.

"I can't sing," I tell him.

"Neither can I," he says. "That's what makes karaoke so fun."

"Promise you won't hold it against me if we get booed off the stage," I tell him.

"I promise," he says. "Do you like Carrie Underwood?"

"I *love* Carrie Underwood," I say. I've never listened to Carrie Underwood.

"Cool. Want to do 'Jesus, Take the Wheel'?"

"Why not?"

"Guys aren't supposed to sing duets," Randall says. I can tell he thinks it's akin to making out in public.

"Have you ever heard of Simon and Garfunkel?" Rhonda asks him.

"I don't listen to hip hop," says Randall.

"They're not . . . forget it," she sighs and rolls her eyes.

Paul and I are the first to perform. Paul wasn't kidding when he said he couldn't sing. He's not only got a terrible voice, but he's also tone deaf.

"Get off the stage," I hear Rhonda shout at us. But Paul only sings louder.

"That was fun," Paul says when the song is over.

"I can't believe you made me do that," I say. "We were so bad, I could hear wolves howling for us to stop."

"You're funny," Paul punches me on the shoulder. "Sorry I was such a grouch earlier. I don't like being woken up."

"I'll remember that for the future."

"Are you okay? You're sweating."

"It's really hot in here."

"Want to go outside for some fresh air?"

"With you?"

"I could find Randall if you'd rather go with him," Paul says with a sly smile.

"No! I mean . . . I don't know what I mean."

"Let's just go outside."

Paul leads me out to the deck that circles the lodge. I lean against the railing and look up at the sky.

"The stars look close enough to touch," I say.

"They're incredible aren't they? I feel like Columbus crossing the Atlantic with nothing but the stars to guide him," Paul says.

"I wish I could use my astrology app to see which stars these are," I say.

"There's Mars," Paul says, pointing to the sky.

"Where?" I ask him.

Paul comes up next me and levels his arm with my eyes. I stop breathing. He's so close to me, I can feel the heat from his body.

"See that big red dot? That's it there. And see that there? That's the International Space Station."

A moment of silence is broken by Randall's voice. "There you guys are! I've been looking all over for you!" Paul and I jump apart. "What are you doing out here?"

"Paul was just showing me the International Space Station," I say.

"Where?" asks Randall.

"That really bright star there," I tell him, pointing to it.

Randall looks up to the sky and frowns. "That's a plane."

I'm about to correct to him, but Paul shakes his

head. I like the idea that he wants to keep it between the two of us.

"Come on back inside," Randall says. "The icebreaker is almost over."

We follow him back into the lodge. My head is spinning a little. It might be the elevation or the fresh air. Or maybe I'm starting to get a crush on Paul.

06

Top of the World

THE NEXT MORNING AT SEVEN, Brian walks up and down the hall. He bangs a pot with a wooden spoon and yells for us to get out of bed.

"If this is how every day here is going to start," Martin says, "I'm going to kill Brian. I mean seriously murder him — they will take me out of here in handcuffs."

"Someone needs a cup of coffee," Randall singsongs.

"There is not enough coffee in the world to wake me from this nightmare," Martin says.

We spend the next half hour waiting our turns to use the bathroom. I'm starving by the time I'm dressed in my khakis and polo. But we have Prayer Circle before we can eat. I'm hangry (hungry and angry at the same time) by the time I'm able to get to the mess hall for a tray of food.

As soon as we sit down, Martin pulls out a case from his pocket. He pricks his finger with the small machine from the case. Then he dabs a strip of paper on a tiny bubble of blood.

"Gross! What are you doing?" Randall says.

"I'm checking my blood sugar," Martin says. "I'm diabetic."

"Do you have to do that while we're eating?" Randall says.

"It's not like I'm breastfeeding," Martin says. "If I knew the Prayer Circle was going to be so long, I would have done it in our room."

"Why do you have to make everyone around you

as miserable as you are?" Randall asks him — like it's his fault he's diabetic.

"You sound like my grandmother," Martin says. "At least she was forced to become an angry Christian in school. What's your excuse?"

"It's only breakfast," Paul says to them. "You two have all day to bicker."

"He started it," Randall drops his eyes and speaks into his cereal.

"So, what's on the agenda for today?" I ask.

"There's a hike this afternoon," Paul says.

That could be fun, especially with Paul. "I've been wanting to do some sketches of the view from up here."

"You're an artist?" Paul asks.

"More of an illustrator. I want to write graphic novels someday."

"I love graphic novels!" Paul's eyes light up. "Do you read manga?"

"When I can get my hands on them. My parents think they're porn. I work part-time at Indigo, so I have access to all sorts of comics. It's one of the reasons I applied to work there."

"So you're reading porn behind your parents' backs?" Randall says.

"Manga isn't porn, it's art," Paul tells him.

"Give me a break. The women in those things are sluts in Catholic school uniforms," Randall says.

I wonder how he would know.

"Where can I buy these books?" Martin says, perking up.

"I rest my case," Randall says.

"Well I think it's awesome that you want to be an illustrator," Paul says, turning from the Randall and Martin show. "I would love to see your drawings some time."

"For sure," I say. I'd better get drawing some scenery.

"So who is up for that hike?" he asks.

"Count me in," I say.

"Me too!" Randall pipes up.

"Really?" Paul, Martin, and I ask him at the same time.

"Why do you seem so surprised?" Randall asks.

"You just don't seem like the hiking type," Paul replies.

"What's that supposed to mean?" Randall asks.

"You look brittle," Martin says. "I've seen clothes hangers with more meat on them than you."

"Well, I'll show you guys," Randall says. "Now if you'll excuse me, I need to get ready for the hike."

Once Randall is out of earshot, Martin muses, "That guy needs to masturbate more."

I feel kind of guilty about the way we treat him. "Do you think we're being too hard on him?"

"He's a piece of work, that one," Paul says. "I'm as religious as they come. But even I can appreciate a good manga."

"We have four more weeks in a room together. Shouldn't we at least try to get along?" I ask.

"Okay, Adam of Green Gables," Martin says, getting up from the table.

"Anne of Green Gables was motivated by beauty, goodness, and imagination," Paul says. "The world would be a much better place if more people were like Anne of Green Gables."

I feel my cheeks go hot at the compliment. Please God, don't let Paul and Martin see me blushing. This is getting weird. I came here to escape being attracted to boys and now I'm mooning over my roommate.

During the hike, I make a point of putting as much space between Paul and I as possible. Paul spends most of the hike walking with Randall while I hang near the rear of the pack with Martin.

"It really is pretty up here," Martin says, taking in the view.

"It's spectacular all right."

"Sorry for being a jerk in the mess hall. I can't control it sometimes."

"I can tell you don't want to be here. I feel the same way."

"It's not the camp. This is how I always feel. I've been clean and sober for a month now. I'm still getting used to experiencing my feelings without the hooch."

"We all have our demons."

"I just wish I knew how to feel joy."

"You will, Martin. Give it time."

We come to a halt at the top of a peak.

Becky, our guide, says, "Let's take this moment to appreciate God's creation."

We stand silently, the wind blowing across our faces. All of a sudden, someone starts singing 'Top of the World.' Martin and I look to see who is singing. It's Paul. His voice is full of love and joy, nothing like his singing voice from karaoke. It's beautiful. The other hikers begin to sing along with him. I join in. I imagine our voices rising through the mountains to God's ears.

Paul and I lock eyes and smile at each other while we sing. Paul's face is like his voice, filled with love and joy. I feel like Paul and I are close enough to touch, even though all the rest of the hikers are standing between us.

I look away to break the spell. The more I feel for Paul, the more I need him to like me back. Am I confusing his love of God with feelings he might have for me? I need to stop deluding myself. Paul is too Christian to be gay. But I can't stop thinking about him. What am I going to do?

07

Landline

THE ONLY PHONE THE CAMPERS can use is in a tiny office near the mess hall. It's made of hard black plastic, with a phone number typed onto a round piece paper glued to the centre of an actual dial. We have to sign up to get thirty minutes of phone time. A counsellor sits outside the open office door to make sure you're not up to anything.

"Do you know how to use that thing?" Brad says.

"I think I can figure it out," I tell him.

"Do you know your home phone number?"

"Yes. I'm not an idiot."

"A lot of campers don't know their home phone numbers," Brad says. "I'll be right outside. If I suspect you're up to no good, I'll come in and hang up the phone."

"I'll be good. I promise," I put my finger in the round hole and push the dial around. It's harder to dial than I thought it was going to be. How did people do this back in the day?

"Hello?" Mom says.

"Hey, Mom, it's me, Adam."

"What a pleasant surprise. I was wondering how you were doing." She sounds like she wishes she hadn't picked up the phone.

"How are things?" I ask.

"Quiet. It's a blessing after the, um, stress of the last little while. I've been praying a lot, which has been a comfort."

"How's Dad doing?"

"He's okay, I guess. He's still a little tense."

"Can I speak to him?"

"I don't know if that's such a good idea. It might be best to give him a little more time."

"Okay."

"How about you? Do you feel any . . . better?"

"I do. Pastor Connell was right. I did need some time away alone. Thanks again for the sketchbook. I've been drawing the scenery like crazy."

"That's nice. It's beautiful up there, is it?"

"Words can't describe it. I wish I had my phone so I could send you pictures. You would get dizzy just looking at them."

"How are they are treating you?"

I can feel Mom dancing around the real reason I'm here. If she had her way, we would never again speak about me being gay. At this point, I'd like that too. But I don't think Dad would ever let us forget.

"I've met a lot great people. I've even managed to have some fun between Prayer Circles and Bible Study."

"Are they feeding you well?"

"The food is actually pretty good. I've been impressed with the whole set up. Where did you and Dad find the money to send me here?"

"We used your university fund."

"Are you out of your mind?" I get out of the chair and start to pace as far as the phone cord will let me.

"You didn't expect us to spend $5,000 of our own money, did you?"

"But that's *my* money. I earned it and gave it to you to put into my education fund. We had a deal."

"I don't know why you're getting mad at me. You brought this on our family. I'm still dreading running into Greta Harris at church on Sunday."

"I need to go. I can't take this anymore."

"Adam, you have to take responsibility for what you did to our family!"

"The only thing I did was tell you the truth."

"Is that what you think? You have been keeping this secret for who knows how long. And out of the blue you lie about where you are and flaunt yourself in a shopping mall where everyone can see. It was only a matter of time before something like this happened."

"Mom, I have to get off the phone before I say something we'll both regret."

"Let me save you the effort," Mom says. She hangs up the phone.

I drop the phone on the base and walk out of the office. There is so much tension in my neck and shoulders I can barely turn my head to respond when Brad asks if I'm okay.

"I'm fine," I tell him. "Just a little misunderstanding with my mother."

"I'll say. If I spoke to my mother like that, she would have washed my mouth out with soap."

I start to tell him to mind his own business. But I think better of it. Instead I go back to the room. No one is there. I grab my sketchbook and pencil out from under my pillow and sit by the window. I try to draw the horizon, but all that comes out of me are images of storm clouds and tornadoes.

"I thought I saw you coming this way," a voice says from behind me. I dread that it might be Randall, but it's Paul. "They're showing *The Sound of Music* in the media room. Want to come?"

"No thanks. I think I'm going to turn in early."

Paul leans over to see what I'm sketching. "Whoa. Is everything okay?"

"It's nothing."

"Those sketches don't look like nothing," Paul says. "You know, you can talk to me, Adam. I promise not to judge."

"It's my parents. We're not getting along at the moment. It's stressing me out."

"Is that why you're here?"

"Yeah, it is."

"Do you want to tell me what's wrong?"

"It's personal."

"I understand."

"What about you? Do you get along with your parents?"

"Like a house on fire."

"Then why are you here? It seems like everyone I've met so far is a little damaged somehow. Not you

SAME LOVE

though. It's like you're the perfect Christian kid that we're all supposed to aspire to be."

"That's the problem. I have great parents who I can talk to about anything, and my sister and I are like best friends. I couldn't be more blessed. Something is still missing though. I can't put my finger on what it is."

"I feel like such a jerk. Here I am feeling sorry for myself and you're as lost as I am."

"That's why we're here: to work out our problems." Then Paul smiles. "But even God took a break on Sunday. What do you say we take our mind off our problems with some Julie Andrews?"

"You're really into *The Sound of Music*, aren't you?"

"You have no idea. I cry at the end every time. Besides, if you don't come I'm going to get stuck listening to Martin and Randall bicker for three hours. Life is too short for that. What do you say?"

"I hate *The Sound of Music*."

"Oh come on. Do it for me," Paul holds out his hand.

"Fine," I give Paul my hand and he pulls me out of the chair. He's stronger than I thought he would be — I barely need to use my legs to stand up. I wish we could hold hands all the way to the media room. But that would fly in the face of the rules in the camp handbook. I've already had enough heartache for one night.

08 Tough Talk

ALL CAMPERS HAVE TO SIGN UP for one session of Tough Talk a week. Tough Talk is where we discuss our feelings, doubts about our life, and faith in God. If we "forget" to sign up, one of the counsellors will sign up for us. Martin has already been caught trying to get out of it.

Rhonda is alone in the common area when I show up for the session. I've been dying to talk to her in private, but we're always doing some stupid activity or Randall is hanging off my shirttail.

"How goes it?" I ask as I take a seat next to her on the couch.

"I totally got caught falling asleep in Bible Study this morning," she says.

"I hate that. Who was running the session?"

"Becky."

"No wonder. Sometimes I want to throw water in her face to liven her up. Wait till you have it with Brad. That guy will give you nightmares."

"I'm convinced Becky's having a lesbian affair with Tania."

"You're making that up."

"Maybe, but I've been spreading the rumour in case it's true."

"Gossip is a sin, Rhonda."

"You can't go to hell for what you don't believe in."

I've been aching to talk to someone about how I feel about Paul. Now's the time. "Speaking of hell, can I tell you a secret?"

"Always."

I look around to make sure we're still alone. "I think I have a crush on one of my roommates."

"Get out!" Rhonda says. "Please tell me it's not that Jesus freak from the icebreaker."

"Randall? Blech. No, it's Paul, the Asian guy."

"The one with the boy-band haircut?"

"That's him."

"He has great shoulders!"

"He does, doesn't he? He's a total sweetheart. He's like the nicest guy I've ever met. And not only that, he's super smart and knows everything about movies and books."

"You should marry him," Rhonda says.

"I don't even know if he's gay. He's pretty religious."

"So? You're the most religious gay I've ever met."

"Yeah, but Paul really believes. He prays all the time in our room and reads the Bible like it's *Harry Potter*."

"The Bible is *Harry Potter* as far as I'm concerned."

"I wish you would stop beating up on religion. It's not helping me sort out how I feel."

"It's not the *message* I have a problem with, it's the messenger," she says.

"If I could be gay and Christian, I wouldn't be in this mess."

Rhonda pinches my leg.

"Ow! What did you do that for?" I rub the spot, but look up when I realize someone has come into the room.

"Hey, Rhonda, what's shaking?" Paul says, smiling down at us.

I try to speak but no words come out.

"Nothing but my perky breasts!" Rhonda answers, giving a demonstration.

"Is there room for one more?" Paul asks.

"Have a seat," Rhonda scoots over to make room on the couch for him.

"I feel like I haven't talked to you since the icebreaker," Paul says to her. "How are you enjoying camp so far?"

"I still hate my roommates. Although I did make a pretty cool ashtray in arts and crafts the other day. Too bad I don't smoke." Rhonda nudges me as she asks Paul, "How about you?"

"I've been enjoying myself a lot. It's been great getting to know Adam," Paul smiles again. "Did he tell you he's been teaching me how to draw?"

"No, he didn't!"

"He's pretty good," I tell her.

"Everything I draw looks like I did it with my left hand," Paul says. "And I'm right-handed."

"You're too hard on yourself," I tell him.

"I'm being honest with myself," Paul says. "I'll never be the artist you are, Adam. I do find it to be relaxing though."

"You two sound like an old married couple," Rhonda says with an evil grin.

That brings the conversation to a screeching halt.

The common area starts filling up with more campers. Soon there is no more room on the couches and people have to sit on the floor.

"Sorry I'm late," Brian says, rushing in with his ever-present clipboard. "I got my sessions confused and went to the wrong part of the lodge."

As always, we start the session off with a quick prayer. Then Brian says, "Who would like to start us off?"

Paul raises his hand.

"Please come forward, Paul," Brian says. "Before Paul begins, I would like to remind everyone there is to be no judging or cross-talk when another camper is speaking. Tough Talk is about being open and honest with each other."

Paul sits cross-legged in the middle of the common area. His head is down.

"A couple of days ago I was telling my bunkmate about how everyone thinks I have this perfect life, but that I feel something is missing," Paul starts.

"And how does that make you feel?" Brian asks him.

"Guilty . . . confused," Paul answers.

"Those are normal feelings, Paul," Brian says. "You can't let them interfere with your faith."

"I know. But I feel like I've been on this quest for something in my life that's been missing. It's like when you can't find your keys: You can see exactly where they are in your head, and when you go to get them they're not there."

"Amen to that," Rhonda says.

"Rhonda, please," Brian says sternly. "Continue, Paul."

"The thing is, after the conversation with my bunkmate, it was like something clicked in my brain. I felt like the answer to my problem was staring me in the face. It was so close it was like I could reach out and touch it. The only problem is, I'm not sure it's what I want."

"Do you feel comfortable telling us about it?" Brian asks.

Rhonda squeezes my hand.

"Not really," Paul says. "I will say that this *thing* goes against everything I've been taught to believe."

"We can't control when God decides to test our faith, Paul," Brian tells him. "But we must rise to the challenge."

"But I don't want be tested!" Paul seems annoyed with Brian. Or is it with me? "Things were perfectly fine the way they were. I don't deserve this."

"What you're experiencing is a natural part of being a Christian," Brian looks up at all of us. "The key is to pray and avoid temptation."

"I'll try," Paul says.

For the next hour the other campers take turns talking about the challenges they face being Christian in a secular world. One person tells us about her terrible relationship with her mom. Another talks about his run-ins with the law. One guy tells us about the time he thought about setting fire to his church. We all look at each other nervously.

I stop paying attention after a while. All I can think about is Paul's confession. I wish I didn't know he was struggling with his faith. Before he said anything, I could write off whatever I'm feeling for him as being one-sided and all in my head. Now, I'm not so sure.

uno

"UNO!" RANDALL SHOUTS, placing a red card on the table.

"Agh!" Martin takes another card from the pile.

"How can you not have a five or a red card?" Paul asks Martin as he decides which card to play.

"Because God is out to get me," Martin says, his face hidden behind a fan of UNO cards.

"Don't blame God. You're just lousy at UNO," Randall taunts him. He holds his last card to his chest, as if he can feel the victory.

"Green," says Paul, placing a wild card on the pile.

It's games night and the mess hall is filled with campers playing board and card games. Brian and Becky are supposed to be supervising us, but they're just sitting quietly reading their Bibles.

"Pick up four!" I say, playing my card.

"Crap!" Randall says.

Paul laughs and Randall shoots him a nasty look. Paul's face suddenly becomes serious, hiding any trace of joy at Randall's expense. But I can see Paul's little grin out of the corner of my eye. I'm sandwiched between Randall and Paul. My knee is a few inches away from Paul's, and I can feel the heat of his skin coming through his khakis.

"I hate this game!" Martin says, picking up another card. "I wish they had Cards Against Humanity or something fun."

Paul puts another green card down on the pile. "They should make a Christian Cards Against Humanity."

I put down another card, and hide my remaining two cards in my palm.

"Christian or not, Cards Against Humanity sounds vulgar," Randall says. He plays his card and spreads the remaining four so he can see them.

"That's what makes it fun," Martin tells him. Martin finally puts a card down, followed by Paul.

"Miss a turn!" I say, putting another card down.

"You guys are out to get me!" Randall accuses.

"Awesome!" Martin plays another card and pumps his fist in the air. This is the most energized he's been since he got here.

"I'm not here to make friends," I smile.

"Adam, you sound like you're on one of those reality shows," says Paul. He looks at his hand and then picks up a card.

"Now *you're* being vulgar," I say. Paul smiles at me. He seems to enjoy it when I tease him.

Truth be told, Randall is right. I have been out to get him during the game. It's like I've been taking out all my anger at my parents, Greta, and Michelle Harris on him. And it feels really good.

I get the feeling Paul wants to keep Randall from

winning as much as I do. The moment it looks like Randall is about to win a hand, one of us manages to sting him by reversing the direction or changing the colour so he can't put down his last card. It's like we know what's in each other's hands without looking at them. It's kind of freaky.

"Speaking of friends, I feel like the only time I've seen you guys this week is at meals and lights out," says Paul.

"That's the counsellors' way of preventing a revolt. They divide and conquer," explains Martin. "My people have been down this road before."

"That's nuts!" says Randall. "They just don't want us forming bonds that could get us into trouble."

"I thought the point of going to camp was to make friends," I say.

"Spare me. What are the odds of us ever seeing each other when this is over?" Martin asks.

"I was planning on staying in touch with you guys," Paul says. "Weren't you, Adam?"

"For sure," I try not to sound flustered. "Plus there's always Facebook."

"Facebook friends aren't the same as real friends," Martin says.

"My parents don't let me use Facebook," Randall says.

What a relief. That's one friend request I won't have to decline.

"Pick up two, Randall." I say as I lay down the card.

Paul giggles. His laughter warms my heart.

"Not funny, Paul," Randall says.

"It's pretty funny from where I'm sitting," says Martin.

"What do you know about humour? You've spent the last week and a half moping around the lodge like someone ran over your dog," says Randall.

"Don't disrespect my journey," Martin puts his cards down. "You don't know anything about me."

"Oh . . . poor Indian kid with diabetes. The world treats you like a second-class citizen on your reservation — boo-hoo," Randall pretends to wipe tears from his eyes.

"Randall, that's uncalled-for," Paul says.

"I'm so tired of people feeling sorry for themselves. God helps those who help themselves," Randall says.

"It's not my fault my mother left and never came back," Martin says. "And it's not my fault my grandmother wants me to believe in a religion that has done nothing but ruin my culture for the last two hundred years. And for your information: I'm not poor. And I don't live on a *reserve*. That's what they're called in Canada."

Brian knocks on our table and says, "Is everything okay here?"

The four of us look at each other like we're covering up a crime.

"Everything is fine," Martin says. "The game is getting a little intense."

"Martin, what have I been telling you?" Brian asks.

"Give your anger to Jesus," Martin mumbles.

"Exactly. There is nothing life can give you that you and Jesus can't work out together," Brian walks away and Martin gives him the finger behind his back. Paul puts his hand on Martin's wrist and lowers it to the table. I look at Paul's hand on Martin's wrist and feel a flush of jealousy.

"Whose turn is it?" I ask.

"Mine," says Paul. He puts his next card on the table.

"UNO!" I say, putting down my second-to-last card.

We go around the circle again, and I put down my last card to win the hand.

"I win," I say.

"High five!" Paul says. He holds out his hand for a high five. But instead, we hook our thumbs together and flutter our fingers like a bird's wings.

The contact feels good, even if it's just a silly handshake. This is the closest I've felt to anyone since I went shopping with Mike.

"Give me your cards so I can add up the score." Randall is pissed off. Martin and Paul push their cards towards him and he flips them over. "You had a pick up four, Paul! Why didn't you use it to keep Adam from winning the game?"

"I must not have seen it," he says.

Randall's glare chills me to the bone. His eyes seem to say, "I'm on to you two."

I move away from Paul.

10 Bishop's Office

"RISE AND SHINE! Rise and shine!" Brian yells, banging his pot with a wooden spoon. I hear Paul and Martin groan at the same time I do. I see Paul sit up in his bed. He looks around the room like he doesn't know where he is, and then plops back onto his pillow.

"No dawdling!" Brian steps right into our room and bangs the pot over our heads.

"You're giving me a headache," Martin says.

"Adam, Bishop would like to see you in his office after breakfast," Brian says.

That can't be good. "What for?"

"You'll find out when you see him," Brian says. "Do you know where his office is?"

"No."

"It's just down the hall from the media room," Randall pipes up. "It's clearly indicated on the map in your handbook."

"Thanks, Randall." Brian shoots Randall a look like they know something we don't. "See you in the mess hall."

"I wonder what that's about," Paul says.

"I hope everything is okay at home," I say.

"I wouldn't worry too much," Randall says. "Bishop probably wants to see how you're doing."

"What's that supposed to mean?" I ask.

"Nothing," Randall tries to look innocent.

"Why am I not convinced?" I say.

"Because you're smart," Martin says.

All through breakfast I replay the last week in

my mind. What could I have done wrong? I haven't been acting really gay, as far as I can tell. I've been doing my best to keep my crush on Paul to myself. Or have I?

I go straight to Bishop's office from the mess hall. Whatever is going on, I want to get this over and done with before all the guessing drives me crazy.

"Come in," Bishop calls to my knock on the door.

I poke my head inside. Bishop's office is also his bedroom. He is sitting at an old desk that is right up against a single bed.

"Have a seat," Bishop points to the bed. It's the only other place to sit.

This is the first time I've been alone with Bishop. He smells like a combination of body odour and body spray. It prickles my nose.

"Have a seat," he says again. I take a seat on the bed, and look for the closest exit in case he tries to get physical with me.

"Brian said you wanted to see me," I break the silence.

"I wanted to check in and see you how you're doing."

"Have I been acting like something is wrong?"

"Your parents and pastor were very concerned about your spiritual well-being when they arranged for you to come here."

"What did they tell you?"

"They said there was an incident with a gay student from your school."

"Mike is just a friend. We were only shopping."

"Boys aren't supposed to go shopping together."

"People keep saying that to me. I work in a mall, and I see guys shopping together all the time."

"I'm only bringing it up because you're sharing a room with three other boys. I worry that it might be tempting for you."

"In what way?"

"I think you know what I'm talking about."

"No, I don't," I say. I'm going to make him say it. "Please explain it to me."

Bishop shifts in his office chair. I can tell he was

hoping our conversation wouldn't come to this.

"It's been brought to my attention that you're very close to one of your roommates."

"Martin? I'm concerned about him. He's obviously depressed, and the diabetes can't help."

"I'm talking about Paul."

"We're just friends."

"You said you were 'just friends' with this homosexual from school. Yet you lied to your parents so you could be with him."

"They wouldn't understand. They *didn't* understand."

"Can you blame them, after you told them you think you're gay?"

"I haven't done anything wrong — with Mike *or* Paul."

"Not yet, but that doesn't mean you won't."

"I am trying to be the best Christian I can be. Everyone keeps acting like I'm fast and loose with my morals when I'm not. Do you have any idea what this has been like for me?"

"Yes I do," Bishop says.

I can hear in his voice he is telling the truth. I'm too surprised to speak.

"I too am a straight man trapped in a homosexual body," Bishop goes on.

"Do my parents know this?" I ask. "Does Pastor Connell?" It doesn't make sense. Why send me here if Bishop is gay himself?

"I try to keep it under the radar as much as possible. It makes some people uncomfortable."

It's making *me* uncomfortable. But now I have to know what Bishop's deal is. "So what did you do?" I ask.

"Like your parents, my parents recognized the problem. They sent me to a doctor who specializes in correcting this sort of behaviour."

"Isn't that illegal?"

"It is in some parts of the country. This happened twenty years ago, before the mainstream media began promoting the gay agenda."

"And this doctor was able to convert you? He

made you straight?"

"Let's say that I learned to control those impulses. And now I have a lovely wife. Someday soon we plan to adopt a child and raise him or her to be a good Christian. I'm living as Jesus expects us to."

"But you still find men attractive."

"The way a man finds another man's wife attractive. And you know the commandment against acting on that."

"But if you're still attracted to men, what's the point?"

"Salvation. You have to learn to control your impulses. Only then will you see God's light. And it's such a beautiful light. So, how have your *urges* been since you've been with us?"

"Urges?"

"Your feelings for other boys."

"I'm aware that I'm not supposed to be attracted to boys. I can't always control what I feel though. It just sort of happens."

"That's to be expected."

"Then why do I feel in my heart that's it wrong to deny who I am?"

"*Feelings* are not good for you, Adam. *Feelings* are what get us into trouble. It's actions that count."

"You have to believe me that I've tried to make this go away. Prayer doesn't work. I even tried to train myself to be straight by masturbating to women on the Internet. It doesn't work."

"Masturbation is a sin."

"See, I can't win!"

"My point is that you can't expect to make yourself normal on your own. You wouldn't expect a drug addict to become sober without going into recovery, would you?"

"I don't know if I would compare being gay to being addicted to drugs."

"Both end in death and destruction. If you let me, I can help you overcome your feelings."

"But if I try to change who I am, won't I damage myself in the process?"

"I don't want to *change* you. I want to help you

SAME LOVE

discover who you really are. I know it feels like you are at war with your body, but you are really at war with God. I'm here to negotiate peace. Will you let me try to help you?"

I think for a second. This goes against everything I've read about being gay. If I decide to go along with this, I might do real damage to myself. But what choice do I have? I'm stuck on the top of this mountain with Bishop for another couple of weeks.

"Okay," I finally say.

"I'll schedule some time with you this week, okay?"

"Thanks, Bishop."

As I walk down the empty hall, I can't stop thinking about what Bishop said. *Feelings are bad for us.* But what is the point of morals without feelings to guide them? If you need God to tell you the difference between what is right and wrong, are you saved? It's enough to send you off the deep end!

When I get back to our room, I see Randall in his bed reading the Bible. He looks at me and smiles. Paul's bed is empty. It dawns on me that Randall must have had something to do with my meeting with Bishop. That would explain the look he shared with Brian this morning. No wonder he's been all over me since I got here. Randall is Bishop's little gay spy.

11 Gossip

IT'S POURING RAIN. The counsellors have been scrambling all day to move all the outdoor activities inside. We've been trapped in the lodge for more than five hours and everyone is starting to get cabin fever. You can have only so many Prayer Circles and play only so many card games before people are ready to snap.

The four of us head back to our room after lunch. We are waiting out the rain on our bunks.

"Do you have to breathe so loud?" Martin asks Randall.

"I'm breathing like I normally do," Randall tells him.

"No you're not. It's like there's something in your nose," Martin says. "Can you guys hear what I'm talking about?"

Paul looks at me from across his bunk and rolls his eyes. "I don't know what you're talking about," he says.

"See," Randall says from the bunk below me. "Stop stirring the turd."

"Maybe you should blow your nose," Martin says.

Randall just snorts in reply.

"What are you drawing, Adam?" Paul asks me.

"Just the room," I tell him.

"Can I come over and see?" he asks.

I would love nothing better than to have Paul sit next to me in bed. But as romantic as it sounds, the last thing I need is for Randall to report back to Bishop. I can hear him say that I was cuddling with

Paul as we listened to the sound of the rain against our window.

"I'm really comfortable here," I lie. "Do you mind if I just chill out by myself for a little bit longer?"

"For sure. No problem." Paul sounds rejected. I feel horrible.

There's a knock on the open door.

"Anyone want to use the phone to pass the time?" Brian says.

"I do!" I say, hopping off my bunk.

"I thought you were comfortable where you were," Paul says.

"I need to ask my mom something," I tell him.

"I thought you were mad at your mom." Paul knows something is up.

If only I could tell Paul we have a spy in our room. If I did: a) I doubt he would believe me, and b) it would mean admitting I have a crush on him.

"Geez Paul, let the guy call his mother for crying out loud," Randall says. For once Randall's meddling is working for me, and not against me.

I follow Brian to the office. I realize that I don't want to actually speak to my parents. Brian unlocks the door and lets me in. I take a seat in front of the phone.

Becky runs up to where Brian is standing, just inside the door. "Brian, can you help us with the karaoke machine in the mess hall. We can't get it to work."

"Can it wait?" Brian asks. "I was about to let Adam use the phone."

"But it's the middle of the afternoon," Becky says.

Brian lowers his voice and says, "I had to give them something to do. I could hear them bickering from my room."

"I can hear you," I say.

Brian turns around. At least he has the decency to look embarrassed.

"If I trust you with the phone, do you promise not to do anything stupid?" he asks.

"What's the worst that can happen?" I ask him.

"Brian, if we don't get that karaoke machine going soon we're going to have a mutiny on our hands," Becky says.

"Oh all right," Brian says. "Adam, don't you dare close this door. Come and get me as soon as you're finished."

"Cross my heart and hope to die." I draw a cross across my chest, like I'm a little kid.

I wait to make sure Brian and Becky are gone before I lift the handset off the receiver and dial.

"Please pick up, please pick up . . ." I whisper. The phone rings once, twice, and then three times. Then . . .

"Whatever you're trying to sell me, I'm not interested," I hear Mike say into my ear.

"Mike! It's Adam, don't hang up."

"Adam? What happened to you? You dropped off the face of the earth. I went by your work to see how things turned out and they said you quit."

"My parents sent me to a Christian camp."

"That sounds horrible. How are you holding up?"

"Not bad, all things considered."

"I feel like this is my fault. We should have been more careful about where we hung out. I'm sorry,

Adam, I didn't mean for this to happen."

"Don't blame yourself. It was only a matter of time before my parents found out the truth. I couldn't keep it a secret forever."

"Where are they hiding you?"

"At an old ski lodge in the mountains north of Squamish."

"It sounds so Disney princess. Maybe a handsome prince will come rescue you."

"I have enough boy problems as it is."

"Please tell me you fell in love at Christian camp. That would make my year."

"Love might be too strong a word. I do have a crush on one of my roommates though. Then another of my roommates snitched on me. And now the camp leader is trying to help me pray the gay away."

"Girl, that can really screw with your head."

"Don't call me *girl*."

"This is not the time for that! Do you need me to come get you? I'm sure my parents would be more than willing to help."

"I'm fine for the moment. He's mostly just counselling me on how to control my urges."

"Is it working?"

"No."

"Good. Don't let them change you, Adam. God loves you just the way you are."

"I thought you don't believe in God."

"I don't, but I do believe in Lady Gaga. And if she says God made us this way then it has to be true."

"What if they're right though? What if we are going straight to hell?"

"That's your parents talking, not you. I don't know much about religion, but I know what's natural and what isn't. You don't get to choose your sexuality. It chooses you. And why would you go to hell for something you have no control over?"

"That's easy to say, but what if my parents never accept me?"

"I can't answer that, Adam. I only wish your parents could see the wonderful person that you are."

There's a knock on the door. I nearly drop the

phone. Brian pokes his head into the room and says, "I got the karaoke machine working. How are we doing in here?"

"I'm wrapping up now," I tell Brian. I say into the phone, "I should go, Mom. I can't wait to show you my sketches when I get home."

"Wait! There's something I need to tell you before you go," Mike yells into the phone.

"There's no need to yell," I tell Mike. "Everyone will hear you."

"Sorry," Mike drops his voice to a normal volume. "I ran into Bob in the mall and he told me he saw Michelle Harris. Guess what? She's pregnant!"

"Ugh!" I gasp.

"Is everything okay?" Brian says. I give him the thumbs up.

"That is shocking news," I say into the phone. "I'll make sure to keep her in my prayers. I have to run, Mom. People are waiting to use the phone."

"Call me as soon as you can," Mike says.

"I will, I promise. I love you."

"I love you too. Hang in there *girl*," Mike says.

I hang up the phone.

An evil grin crosses my face as Brian leads me back to our room. I wish I could have been a fly on the wall when Greta learned her saint of a daughter is knocked up. I wonder if she'll get a secret abortion. But the glee I feel quickly wears off. There have been times when all I wanted was to get revenge on Greta and Michelle for creating the mess I'm in. Now that I've had a taste of that revenge, I actually feel kind of sorry for them both.

12 Bible Study

I'VE BEEN AVOIDING PAUL as much as I can for the last three days. But Paul isn't going along with the program. He wants to hang out together more than ever since my talk with Bishop. I still haven't got proof that Randall ratted me out, but I'm convinced of it just the same.

Yesterday Paul asked if I wanted to have lunch with him. I lied and told him I already had plans with Rhonda. When I got to the mess hall, Rhonda was already eating with her roommates and didn't have space at her table for me. Paul ended up eating at a table with people he didn't know. I ate alone. I kept looking over at him while I was eating. He looked as sad as I felt.

But if I'm not careful, Bishop is going to separate Paul and me. At least we get to spend time together if we're sleeping in the same room. I wish I could tell Paul the truth. The truth only seems to get me in trouble.

I get to Bible Study early to snag my favourite spot in the common area. It's a corner seat on the big leather couch that is far away from where the counsellors usually sit.

"Is it okay if I sit here?" Paul asks, standing in front of me. No one else is sitting on the couch. I would look pretty mean if I told him no.

"Have a seat," I scoot over an inch to make sure our legs don't touch.

"Is everything okay?" Paul asks. "I get the feeling you've been avoiding me."

"I've been doing some private counselling with Bishop and it's cutting into my free time."

"What kind of counselling?"

"It's sort of personal."

"Okay. You know you can tell me anything, right?" Paul looks hurt that I don't confide in him. It pains me to make him feel this way.

"I know, but Bishop wants me to keep this between me and him."

"Hey guys," Rhonda says, sinking into the couch next to Paul. "Where have you been, Adam? It feels like I haven't seen you in days."

"He's on a secret mission from God," Paul says, nudging me with his elbow.

"Bishop hasn't recruited you to blow up an abortion clinic has he?" Rhonda asks.

"That's not funny, Rhonda," Paul says.

"Sorry. I just came back from a lecture by Becky and Tania on how not to dress like a slut. Like it's my job to prevent a guy from raping me."

Martin enters the common area. "Is there room

for one more on that couch?"

"Sure. Squeeze in you two," Rhonda says to Paul and me. She pushes Paul up against me to make room for Martin. I can feel Paul's thigh against mine. This is not a good idea.

"What about me?" Randall says.

"You snooze, you lose," Rhonda tells him.

Randall sneers at Rhonda and sits down on the carpet in front the couch.

"I need to check my insulin. I feel light-headed," Martin says. He pulls out his diabetes kit and starts drawing blood.

"Do you need to do that right here?" Randall says.

"Would you prefer I pass out?" Martin asks.

"Okay everyone, find a seat," Brad says. He takes his place in the chair nearest the fireplace. Brad is carrying a Bible with some notes folded inside it. "Martin, would you please open your Bible to 1 Corinthians 7:2 and read the passage for us?"

Martin fumbles with his Bible trying to find the chapter and verse.

"Corinthians is in the New Testament, Martin," Brad says, with a roll of his eyes. Randall giggles at Martin's expense. Paul helps Martin find the passage.

"But because of the temptation to sexual immorality, each man should have his own wife and each woman her own husband," Martin reads softly, almost to himself. It's like he's embarrassed for people to hear his voice.

"Thank you, Martin. Adam, would you please read Hebrews 13:4 for us? Hebrews is in the New Testament as well."

"I know that," I open up my Bible to the passage. Brad is such a jerk. "Let marriage be held in honour among all, and let the marriage bed be undefiled, for God will judge the sexually immoral and adulterous."

"Thank you," Brad says. "Now who can tell me what God is trying to tell us in these passages?"

Randall's hand shoots up like a rocket.

"Randall," Brad says.

"That sex is a sin unless you are married," Randall

says. "And that if people waited to get married before having sex there wouldn't be so many diseases, abortions, and children without both parents."

"Very good, Randall," Brad tells him.

Rhonda puts up her hand.

"Yes, Rhonda," Brad says.

"How do you get all of that from just a couple of sentences?" Rhonda asks.

"Christians have been studying the Bible for hundreds of years," Brad says. "You learn these things after a while."

Rhonda puts up her hand again.

"Yes, Rhonda," Brad says.

"What does Jesus say about sex before marriage?" Rhonda asks.

"He says it stains your soul," Brad says.

"Does he though?" Rhonda says. "I know the quote you're talking about. My understanding of that verse is that evil intentions come from sex and theft and murder and all the other Ten Commandments. But Jesus never comes right out and says sex is a sin."

"She's speaking out of turn," Randall says, with his hand up.

"Fine," Rhonda says. She lifts up her hand and goes on, "I guess what I'm asking is where in the Bible does Jesus talk about sex? And while we're at it, where does he come down on the gays?"

"It's all over the New Testament, stupid," Randall says meanly.

"But where *exactly* does Jesus say God hates gays and sex?" Rhonda asks.

I look over at Paul. He starts to sink into the couch like he's trying to disappear.

"Randall is right, Rhonda. Sex and gays are a sin in God's eyes. It's a no-brainer," Brad tells her.

"But where does Jesus *say* it?" Rhonda says, still holding her hand up. "Isn't he the one we're supposed to be obeying?"

"I don't have an answer for that right now," Brad has to admit. "But I assure you, Jesus frowned upon gays and sex before marriage." He's trying to shut her down.

"His best friend was a hooker!" Rhonda says.

"And you're an expert on that," Randall says.

"I don't need your help, Randall!" Brad says.

"I've looked through the New Testament for some quote from Jesus that says I'm going to hell because I've had sex. Spoiler alert: I can't find it," Rhonda says. "The more I read the Bible, the more it becomes clear to me that Jesus was actually a pretty cool guy. It's the people claiming to speak for him who are trying to oppress women and minorities."

"That's enough, Rhonda!" Brad says.

"I'm tired of being taught to hate myself for who I am," Rhonda continues. "If this really is a Bible Study, then you should be telling us about where the Bible contradicts itself. It's only fair."

"I said enough!" Brad slams his Bible on the coffee table in front of him. "I'm running this study, not you!"

Out of the corner of my eye I can see Paul put his hand on Rhonda's knee to calm her down. Randall puts his hand in the air.

"Put your hand down, Randall," Brad says. "Now everyone open your Bibles to Hebrews 5:8-9: Son though he was, he learned obedience from what he suffered and, once made perfect, he became the source of eternal salvation for all who obey him . . ."

Brad doesn't ask our opinion for the rest of the session. Instead, he tells us what each of the Bible quotes mean. After he dismisses us I pull Rhonda off to the side.

"I think what you said was really cool," I tell her.

"Thanks," she says. "But where were you when I needed someone to back me up? It would be nice if you guys grew a pair instead of rolling over and playing dead."

Rhonda storms off in the direction of the girls' section of the lodge.

13 Do or Die Time

I SKIP DINNER TO GO OUTSIDE and sketch by myself at one of the picnic tables. Between my private prayer sessions with Bishop and being publicly shamed by Rhonda, all I want to do is curl up and die.

I put pencil to paper and look out across the horizon. The sky is a swirl of oranges and blues. Sailboats make little pinpricks on the surface of the ocean. All this beauty and I don't feel connected to any of it. I should be praising God for his gifts, but I feel nothing. It scares me.

"I brought you something to eat," a voice from behind me says.

I turn around to see Paul holding out a sandwich on a plate and a bottle of water.

"You didn't need to do that," I tell him. "I'm not that hungry." But I take the plate and bottle.

"You say that now, but you'll regret it after they close the mess hall for the night."

"Thanks. You're too nice to me." I take a bite of the sandwich and then another. "I guess I was hungrier than I thought."

Paul puts his hand on my arm. "Don't let Rhonda get you down."

I look at Paul's hand on my wrist. The passage from the camp handbook about excessive touching flashes through my mind. I pull my arm away, and pretend to wipe mustard off my face. I can tell Paul isn't fooled.

"Rhonda was right," I tell him. "A real friend would have defended her."

"It's not your battle, Adam."

"It is though. I don't like how the Bible is being taught to us either. I wish I had Rhonda's strength. I'm sick and tired of hiding from my feelings."

"Rhonda will come around. You have to believe that everything is going to be all right in the end. Secret handshake?" Paul holds up his hand.

I want to touch him so much that I almost can't dare to. But if I don't start being my true self now, when will I? Our thumbs lock around each other, and our fingers flutter in the air like the wings of a bird. We stretch our hands up in the air until our arms can't reach anymore.

"I needed that," I tell him.

We sit silently for a couple of minutes. Then Paul says, "Did I do something to offend you? I get the feeling you're avoiding me."

"It's not you, it's me. I've had a lot on mind."

"Does this have anything to do with your private sessions with Bishop?"

"Yeah."

"I wish you would tell me why you're meeting with him. I thought we were friends."

"We are friends. This is different though."

"Different how?"

I want to tell him how I feel, but I'm afraid. Every time I'm honest about my feelings, it ends up making things worse. But Paul is my friend. I can't keep giving him the cold shoulder without some sort of an explanation.

"Let me show you something," I say. I open my sketchbook and flip to some sketches.

Paul looks at the pictures, his eyes widen and soften. He turns the page, absorbing each sketch one at a time.

"These are of me," he says. "When did you draw these?"

"Early in the morning before everyone woke up. Or by the light of the moon through the window when I couldn't sleep."

"Why me? Why not Martin or Randall?"

"I have a crush on you on Paul. Can't you tell?"

"Deep down maybe. But I don't think of myself as attractive to people."

That's exactly one of the reasons I have a crush on him.

"You've done a really good job of hiding your feelings." he says finally.

"Not good enough. Someone told Bishop they suspected I like you as more than a friend. That's why I have to meet with him every day to pray."

"Do you know who told?"

"It had to be Randall. He's the only one who cares enough to say anything."

"That makes the most sense. Do you have proof?"

"What difference does it make? It doesn't change how I feel for you."

"Does that mean the prayer sessions with Bishop aren't working?"

"Do you want them to?"

Paul looks out over the horizon. The wind plays with his hair. I try to focus on how I will draw that later.

"I don't know," he says. "This is so confusing. I thought you didn't like that I was being so clingy."

"I didn't want you to get into trouble because of me."

"I guess I always knew you liked me as more than a friend. I didn't see the harm in it. It's not like we were doing anything bad. No one — girl or boy — has ever had a crush on me before. Not that I know of anyway. I like the way it makes me feel. I like the way *you* make me feel."

"I didn't mean to put you in this position. I didn't mean for this to happen."

"I know."

It's do-or-die time. "How do you feel about me?"

Paul takes a deep breath and looks away. This is not a good start.

"I would be lying if I said I didn't feel the same way," he says.

A weight lifts from my chest. I wish I could hug him, but I'm afraid someone will see us.

"For years now, I've felt a bit off. It was like something in my brain wasn't clicking," Paul continues. "That first night we met and we sang karaoke together it was like all the pieces fell into place."

"You don't know how happy you're making me feel right now," I confess.

"But I don't want to be gay," Paul says.

"But you said you feel the same way about me as I do for you."

"I do. I really do. And it's a relief to finally say it. But this is a sin, Adam."

"Love is not a sin."

"No, but romantic love between two men *is*. I care for you. But my loyalty to God is stronger than my feelings for you. I can't throw away a lifetime of devotion for a teenage crush."

"I never asked you to!" I say. "You asked me why I was avoiding you and I told you the truth. Should I have lied?"

"Let me explain —" he starts.

"You don't need to explain; I understand perfectly! This is typical of Christianity. You tell the truth and then you get shunned or sent away to some stupid camp on the top of a mountain."

"I don't want things to change between us," Paul says.

"Too late for that."

"It's not like we can date while we're here."

"Don't worry. I'm not even sure I like you anymore."

"You would be lucky to have me as boyfriend," Paul says, getting defensive. "I would treat you like a king."

"Well I guess we'll never know for sure will we?"

"No. I guess we won't."

I know I should slam my sketchbook shut and storm back to the lodge. At the same time, I don't want to leave him, not like this. I'm surprised when Paul speaks first.

"Why is it that I'm really mad at you right now, but I want to kiss you?"

All my anger vanishes. We really are feeling the same thing. "Would it make you feel better if I told you I feel the same way?"

"Yes it would."

"Well I do."

"What are we going to do?" Paul asks.

"We *just* admitted our feelings to each other. Maybe if we get to know each other better, we might realize we don't really like each other that much."

"I never thought of it that way."

"The only thing that's changed now is that we've talked about it. Normal couples don't date right away, do they? They wait and see how they feel about each other. Why don't we wait until camp is over. If there are still feelings, we can figure it out from there."

"On one condition."

"What's that?"

"Will you be my date for movie night?"

"I'll pick you up at the foot of your bunk bed."

The screen door of the lodge opens and Martin steps outside.

"There you guys are," Martin says. "Randall has been looking all over for you. He's convinced you're up to something."

"Thanks for the warning," I say.

"Anytime," Martin says.

"We should go back to the room one at a time. You go with Martin," Paul tells me. "I'll catch up with you in a bit."

Paul and I have just made our first date and Randall is already trying to break us up.

4 Straying from the Flock

PAUL AND I have been secretly "dating" for three days now. Had I known having a boyfriend felt this amazing, I would have done it sooner. All through high school I pretended to get excited when friends told me they kissed a girl. Really, I was jealous they got to experience a natural part of being a teenager that I couldn't.

I feel weird describing what Paul and I are doing as *dating*. We haven't kissed yet, but we "accidentally" touch hands or feet when we're close to each other in line at the mess hall or Bible Study. We look into each other's eyes as we sing around the campfire.

The toughest part about being Paul's boyfriend is I want to tell the whole world about it. At the same time, the secrecy makes our relationship special. What we have is just between the two of us. It's not out there on display for people to judge. I want to keep it this way for as long as possible.

We don't think Randall suspects a thing. I've been doing my best to pay extra attention to Randall when the four of us are in the room. I listen to his theories about Jesus and his plans for becoming a pastor. The only person who might be on to us is Martin. Although he's been so depressed lately I don't think Paul and I are really on his radar.

"You seem a lot happier since the first time I saw you," Bishop says when we meet for our session.

"It must be all the fresh air and prayer."

"I told you it would make a new man out of you!" he says.

"I can't believe I doubted you."

"Your parents will be so pleased to hear this."

"What did you say?"

"I was just thinking out loud."

"Are you giving my parents progress reports?"

"Adam, don't be upset. They're concerned for your spiritual well-being. You were very confused when you arrived here. We thought your case required more drastic measures."

"What kind of drastic measures?"

"This is a conversation for you and your parents to have."

"I have a right to know. This is my life we're talking about. I should get some say in it."

"Not until you're eighteen."

"You said yourself I was doing better. What harm would it do to tell me? If anything, you should be encouraging me to keep up this good work I've been doing."

Bishop looks at his hands on his lap. "I was going to recommend your parents send you to a doctor who specializes in helping gay Christians."

"Like the one you saw?"

"Yes. I didn't think it would hurt for you to meet with one. Just to make sure you stay on the path you're on. It's for your own good, Adam. Look at me. I went to one and I couldn't be happier."

If Bishop Andrews is supposed to be the model for happiness, count me out.

There's a knock on the door.

"Bishop, I need to speak to you," Brad says from the other side of the door. "It's urgent."

"Excuse me," Bishop goes to speak with Brad. I hear a series of urgent whispers and then Bishop turns back to me. "Adam, I need you to return to your room as quickly as possible."

"Is everything okay?" I ask.

"Everything is fine," he says, but he sounds flustered. "Something has come up. The counsellors and I need to devote all of our attention to it."

I do as I'm told without another word. Paul, Martin, and Randall are already in the room when I get there. It's like a prison lockdown.

"Do you guys know what's going on?" I ask.

"Rhonda ran away from the camp," Randall says. His face is lit up with excitement.

"What? How?"

"She must have snuck out of her room in the middle of the night. They didn't notice she was gone until after lunch." Trust Randall to know what's going on.

"I wish she'd asked me to come with her," Martin says.

"I hope she's okay," Paul says. "We're in the middle of nowhere."

"I'm sure she used her to body to get some trucker to give her a ride into town," Randall says.

"Or she's *walking* down the mountain," Paul says.

Brian sticks his head into our room. "Hi boys, I need to do a quick head count."

"All present and accounted for," Randall says.

"Good. Now stay here until we call on you," Brian moves onto the next room.

We're confined to our rooms for the better part of the day. During the afternoon session of Tough Talk, Brian takes attendance twice to make sure he hasn't missed anyone. The first person to take the floor is Sarah, Rhonda's roommate.

"I'm really worried about Rhonda," Sarah says. "I haven't been nice to her since we got here. I sort of blame myself that she ran away."

"It's kind of you to care so much for Rhonda," Brian says. "But we're here to talk about *your* soul and *your* faith. It's up to Rhonda to decide if she wants to go to heaven or hell."

For the rest of the Tough Talk session, Brian changes the subject if someone mentions Rhonda's name, even if it's to say a prayer for her safety. During dinner, it's like the counsellors have been coached to act like Rhonda never existed. Rhonda is all the campers want to talk about.

After lights out, I whisper to the others, "Where

do you think Rhonda is right now? Do you think she's okay?"

"I'm sure she's fine," Paul says to me. "She's probably been planning to run away from the day she got here."

"What if she got lost or kidnapped?" I feel even more guilty than Sarah. She was just Rhonda's roommate. I was supposed to be her friend.

"Adam is right," Martin whispers. "My mom disappeared five years ago and no one has seen her since."

"That's different," Randall says.

"How is it different?" Martin asks.

"Don't answer that, Randall," Paul says. "Things are bad enough as it is."

"Do you hear that?" Randall says.

We go quiet for a second. We hear cars approaching the lodge. Brian runs past our room in the dark towards the front entrance. Flashing red and blue lights swirl through the trees outside our window.

The four of us get out of bed and crowd around the open door. We hear the relieved voices of the counsellors thanking police officers and asking if they would like something to eat or drink before they go back out into the night.

We listen some more as Bishop and the counsellors interrogate Rhonda in the common area. Bishop tells her how disappointed and worried they have been. Rhonda doesn't have a chance to say anything in reply before Bishop asks Tania to escort her back to her room.

After Rhonda is gone, we hear Bishop discussing her with Brian, Brad, Tania, and Becky. The only words I can make out are, "Rhonda," "Silence," "Lesson," and "Amen."

We hear Brian's footsteps coming back towards our room. The four of us get back into our beds as quickly and quietly as possible. I breathe as quietly as I can, until I hear Brian enter his room at the end of the hall.

"I told you she would be okay," Paul says, just loud enough for me to hear.

"She sounded miserable," I say.

"She's back here, isn't she?" says Martin.

"She is going to be in so much trouble," Randall says. "This is the best day of my life."

15 Prayer Circle

THE NEXT MORNING, Brian knocks on our door to wake us up. It's a nice change from banging his stupid wooden spoon against a pot.

"Hey guys, I was hoping we could have a little chat before Prayer Circle," he says, taking a seat at the desk by the window. The four of us turn to face him from our beds.

"So I guess you heard the police found Rhonda last night," he starts.

"They did?" Randall says. "We slept right through it."

"Spare Jesus the lie, Randall," Brian says. "I could hear your breathing from the common area."

"Didn't I say you breathe loud?" Martin says to Randall.

"The point is," Brian breaks in, "Bishop wants to send a message to Rhonda that we care for her. But that we're not going to put up with her antics anymore."

"How does he propose we do that?" Paul asks.

"The counsellors are asking all campers not to speak to Rhonda for the next twenty-four hours."

"Can we wave hello?" I ask.

"No. We don't want you to communicate with her at all. No acknowledgement that she is there, even if she asks you to pass the salt in the mess hall. Bishop feels that seeing how it feels to be cast from the flock might bring her to her senses."

"That's kind of harsh isn't it?" I ask.

"That would push me over the edge," Martin says.

"Rhonda gave everyone a scare yesterday. And she may have hurt the reputation of the camp. Her actions can't go unpunished," Brian stands up. "Now can we all agree to this course of action?"

Paul, Randall, and Martin all agree not speak to Rhonda. I just nod my head and move my lips. I can't actually say that I'll do it.

A half hour later we gather outside. Campers are making their way to the Prayer Circle, yawning and wiping the sleep from their eyes. I stand between Randall and Paul. Randall smiles at me and takes my hand. I feel him squeeze it a little as if he's trying to make me feel better.

Paul takes my hand in his. We try not to look at each other for too long in case someone gets suspicious. Prayer Circle is the only time we get to hold hands. That's it for public displays of affection. Martin is on the other side of Paul staring straight ahead at nothing.

I see Rhonda approach the circle. Hands close on each other, locking her out. Rhonda walks around, looking for a spot to join in, like the odd person out in a game of musical chairs. No one lets her in.

I let go of Paul's hand to create a space for Rhonda. Randall yanks on my arm and gives me a nasty look. I match it with one of my own. A moment later I feel Rhonda's hand take mine. Her face is sunburnt. She looks like hasn't slept.

Brad narrows his eyes at me from across the circle. The look on his face reminds me of the one on my father's the day he found out I was shopping with Mike. Brad begins the morning prayer. Before I bow my head, I notice a few mean glances shot my way by the other campers.

"Thank you," Rhonda whispers when the prayer is over.

"Adam! Can I have a word with you?" Brad shouts. He is marching in my direction.

"You better go," I tell Rhonda.

"Don't get into trouble on account of me," Rhonda says.

"Too late."

The next thing I know, Brad has his arm around my shoulder and I'm being led away.

"Didn't Brian tell you not to speak to Rhonda?" Brad asks between gritted teeth.

"He did," I say. "But I felt the Christian thing to do would be to forgive Rhonda. Everyone makes mistakes. Don't you?"

"We'll see what Bishop has to say about this," Brad says.

"What about breakfast?" I ask.

"Breakfast can wait!"

Brad takes me inside the lodge to Bishop's office. He knocks on the door. "Bishop, we have a problem."

"Another one?" Bishop says with a sigh. "Come in."

"Wait here," Brad goes inside alone. Bishop sounds defeated as Brad tells him what happened in Prayer Circle.

"Send him in," I hear Bishop say. Brad holds the door for me. "Have a seat, Adam," Bishop is still in his pajamas. "Now what's this about you speaking to Rhonda?"

132   SAME LOVE

"Bishop, you should have seen the look on her face when we wouldn't let her join the circle. She looked like a puppy at the dog pound."

"That was the point of her punishment!"

"But Jesus tells us to forgive people for their mistakes."

"The time for forgiveness is for Jesus to decide, not you."

"The more I learn about Jesus, the more confused I get. The Bible seems to say one thing. But you, my parents, and my pastor, all say something else."

"We're adults, Adam. We know more about the world than you do. You have to trust us."

"Are you going to tell my parents about this?"

"I have to," Bishop says sadly. "What you did was a sign of weakness. If you can't be trusted to follow one simple rule, how are any of us to believe you can control your urges?"

"It's not the same thing."

"Tell that to your pastor the next time you see him. Something tells me he's going to agree with me.

I'm going to let you off with a warning, but I'll be keeping my eye on you. It's for your own good."

"Thanks, Bishop," Somehow I manage to keep the sarcasm out of my voice.

"You're welcome."

The jerk actually accepted my thanks for not punishing me for being human. The longer I stay here, the more I realize I don't belong.

16 No Good Deed Goes Unpunished

I GRAB A QUICK BITE to eat in the mess hall before it closes for the morning. Then I run back to our room to get ready for the day. Paul, Randall, and Martin are waiting for me.

"Well? What did Bishop say?" Paul asks. "Are you in trouble?"

"He gave me a warning," I tell him.

"Whew," Paul says.

"A warning? That's it?" Randall sounds amazed.

"Were you expecting the firing squad?" Martin asks.

"I was expecting penance or something," Randall says. "What were you doing talking to Rhonda like that? You made us all look bad."

"I've had enough drama for one day," I tell him. "Please leave me alone."

"Randall is right, Adam," Paul says. "Did you think to ask me if it was okay to let Rhonda stand between us? I could have got in trouble too, you know."

"What?" I can't believe what I'm hearing.

"It was like you decided for the both of us and assumed I would be okay with it," Paul says.

"You're right, I did assume you were going to be okay with it," I tell him. "Rhonda is our friend."

"She broke the rules, Adam. She deserved to be punished," he says.

"She feels trapped. You more than anyone should know how that feels!"

"You don't know what I feel."

So that's what this is about. "I couldn't just turn my back on her," I try to explain.

"You didn't have a problem with it in Bible Study," Paul says.

"What's going on here?" Randall says. "I get the feeling you two aren't arguing about Rhonda."

"Mind your own business for a change, Randall," I snap at him.

"I'm getting Brian," Randall runs out of the room.

I turn back to Paul "What is your problem, Paul? You didn't get in trouble and Rhonda didn't even talk to you. All she did was hold your hand and pray."

"I don't like you dragging me into your politics," Paul says. "I don't like being the centre of attention."

"So when you sing karaoke or K-Pop songs at the top of your lungs, you're trying to blend in?" I say.

"Good one, Adam," Martin says.

"Stay out of it, Martin," Paul and I say together.

"Rhonda's life is none of my business," Paul says. "How Bishop and the counsellors treat her is not my fight."

"You don't always to get to pick and choose your battles," I say. "Sometimes you need to be brave, Paul. You can't blindly do what people tell you."

"I *am* in control of my life," he says. "I wasn't sent here by my parents. I am here because I *want* to be here. And if you can't deal with that, then I don't know if we can be friends."

"I thought you were a bigger person than that." I can't hide my disappointment.

"You think what you want to think," Paul says and turns away. He nearly bumps into Brian, who is coming in through the door. Randall is right behind him.

"Is everything okay in here?" Brian asks.

"I need some fresh air," Paul squeezes past him.

"Everything is fine," I tell Brian. "Just a difference of opinion."

"I'll say. I've never seen Paul look so angry," Brian says. "I think you two need some space from each other. I'll make sure you don't have any activities together today."

"Thanks," I say.

Brian leaves. Randall just stares at me. "Aren't you going to apologize to me?" he asks.

"No," I tell him. I grab my sketchbook and leave the room.

"Wait for me!" I hear Martin say behind me.

I try to lose Martin but he catches up with me on the lawn behind the lodge.

"I don't want to be around anyone right now," I tell him.

"I never want to be around people. But here I am," Martin says.

"Please leave me alone."

"I know about you and Paul," Martin says suddenly.

I look around to make sure no one else has heard him.

"What do you mean you know about us?" I whisper

"It's pretty obvious you guys are boyfriends," Martin says.

"Does anyone else know?"

"Randall suspects, but he doesn't have proof. If you plan on keeping it a secret, I would avoid having lovers' quarrels like the one you just had in the room."

"I can't believe that happened."

"You had every right to be mad at Paul," Martin says. "And he had every right to be mad at you. I don't know everything that's going on between you guys. But it doesn't take a genius to see that it's something special."

"Something special that I just screwed up."

"Maybe. It's hard to tell. This is not the ideal place for two guys to start dating each other."

"Tell me about it."

"I'm kind of jealous actually," Martin admits.

"You're gay too?"

"I'm straight as an arrow. But I envy you that whole emotional connection thing. I can't say I've ever had it with anyone. I watch you guys sometimes, the way you make each other happy and I think, 'Why can't I feel that for another person?'"

"I think you're awesome Martin. You're funny and smart. And you always have a quick comeback for anything anyone says to you."

"I know people love me. But why can't I feel it? It's like there's this wall between me and the rest of the world. It's like when you have a cold and you can't taste anything. That's how I go through life."

"Is there anything I can do?"

"If there was I would have asked you a long time ago. Come on," he says. "We should join some group or something before they think we're making out."

"You're not my type," I tell him.

"Don't flatter yourself."

17 Sadie Hawkins

IT'S THE SECOND-TO-LAST Friday before the end of camp. In the counsellors' never-ending efforts to reinforce straight Christian relationships, they have planned a Sadie Hawkins dance. I would be excited by the prospect of going to a dance, but Paul and I have not spoken in two days.

I'm trying not to show how much our argument has affected me. It's hard. I want to tell Paul I'm sorry. But I don't feel like I'm wrong. If anything, he's the one who should apologize to me. At the same time, I'm worried that we're going to go our separate ways without making up. It makes me mad that Paul doesn't understand my point of view, but not so mad that I never want to speak to him again.

Martin, Randall, and I are standing off to the side of the dance floor. We watch boys and girls mingle with one another. Paul is off with some of the other campers.

"Don't look now, but I think Rhonda's roommate is making a move on Paul," Randall says.

"Where?" I say, looking around the mess hall.

"Over there," Randall points to the other side of the room.

I see Paul holding a cup of non-alcoholic punch. He is smiling and chatting with Sarah.

"Since when has Paul ever shown interest in her?" I say out loud.

"If I didn't know better, I would think you were jealous," Randall says.

"I'm not jealous. I just think it's weird that we've

been here for three weeks and Paul has never once tried to talk to her alone."

"That's because he's been too busy hanging out with you," Randall says.

I don't know what I want to do more right now: get between Paul and Sarah or punch Randall in the throat.

Is Paul really into Sarah? I can't blame him after the way I treated him. What if he falls for her? I try to tell myself he's never going to be able to make her happy. I could tell from our "relationship" that he would always have one foot out the door. It was just like being *my* boyfriend. It wasn't like I was asking him to hold my hand in public. I didn't even expect him to kiss me. All I wanted was his undivided attention. I made it too easy for him. He had nothing to lose.

"I love this song," Randall says, swaying to the music.

"You should ask someone to dance," I tell him.

"I don't like any of the girls here enough for that," he says.

"It's three minutes of your life. It's not like you're asking for their hand in marriage," Martin says.

"I wouldn't want to lead anyone on like that," Randall says.

"You're so weird," Martin tells him.

I feel someone tap me on the shoulder. I turn around and see Rhonda. She's holding up a red Solo cup of punch. "Did you drink the Kool-Aid yet?"

"Not yet," I say.

"Want to dance?" she asks.

"I would like nothing better." I let Rhonda grab my hand and drag me to the dance floor.

"I never thanked you for putting your neck on the line for me at Prayer Circle." We are dancing with a foot of space between us. "It took a lot of guts for you to do what you did."

"It was worth it. If I didn't say anything, I would have lost it."

"Sorry I was such a jerk after Bible Study. I shouldn't have taken it out on you. I was mad and you were an easy target."

"You had every right to be mad at me. It was pretty two-faced of me to support you after the fact. And in private."

"Still, it wasn't my place to force you into saying something you weren't comfortable saying. I can't expect everyone to fight my battles for me."

"That's funny. Paul said the same thing to me after I let you into the Prayer Circle."

"You two aren't fighting over me are you?"

"Let's just say my little protest didn't go over so well with him."

"So that's why he's dancing with Sarah."

"Sort of. Yeah."

"Want me to say something to him?"

"No. I don't want to make things worse than they already are."

"You can't let him fall back on his old ways. You guys make such a cute couple."

"You think so?"

"I wish you could see what you guys look like when you're together. It's like there's this energy coming off you that could power a small town. It's magical."

"But he's *so* deep in the closet. It took so long for me to admit who I am. It figures the first person I have feelings for is too afraid to express who he really is."

"You can't force someone to come out of the closet. You have to let them do it on their own."

I think back to working on the yearbook with Mike. He made me feel comfortable even when I didn't know what I wanted from the world. If he had tried to force me to admit to being gay, I still might be trying to fight it.

"Didn't you say a friend of your family outed you?" Rhonda prompts. "Look at the mess that got you into."

I'm horrified at the idea that I might be doing to Paul what Greta did to me.

Rhonda can tell I need a subject change. "Do you know what you're going to do when you leave here?"

"Bishop is going to recommend my parents send me to a 'doctor' who treats queer Christian kids."

"You can't let your parents do that to you."

"I won't. What about you? What are you going to do?"

"Running away doesn't seem to work. I keep getting caught. I'm going to see if there are any government services that can help me legally get away from my parents. I have an aunt my mother doesn't talk to. I'm hoping she'll take me in."

"Are you ready to give up on your parents like that?"

"They gave up on me," she says. "There's no point in fighting anymore. We're not getting anywhere. Speaking of which — hold on tight."

Rhonda swings me around so fast I almost lose my balance. When my head stops spinning, I look up and see Paul dancing with Sarah right beside us.

Paul and I look into each other's eyes. I don't know if I should smile or look away. Another couple dances in between us and I lose sight of him until the song ends. When the song is over, I go back to where I was standing with Martin and Randall. They haven't budged since I left them.

8 One Pair of Footprints

MARTIN HAS BEEN on one of his downers for a day now. He's barely said a word to any of us. He didn't even insult Randall, when he had at least five great chances to do so. We're sitting in Tough Talk together. Randall has just admitted to one of his lame sins. Of course everyone applauds him for being so honest.

"We have ten minutes," Brian says. "Does anyone else want to talk about what's on their mind?"

"I do," Martin puts up his hand. The rest of the

campers are as shocked as I am. Martin has never once said anything in these sessions.

"Come on up," Brian tells him.

Martin steps over the other campers and sits in the middle of the group. He looks down at his hands. There's a second during which I think he's just pulling our legs and he's not going to say anything at all.

"I know I'm not the easiest person to get along with," he finally says. "I don't have a good attitude about things. And I'm not a people person. I've prayed to feel better about myself but nothing works. Sometimes I wonder why I was even born."

"We all feel that way sometimes," Brian says.

"But my grandmother seems to believe my life is a waste. It's like she blames me for my mom disappearing. Yesterday I was talking to her on the phone and she didn't even ask how I was doing. She just wanted to know if I had found Jesus yet. It never occurs to her that I might feel as abandoned by my mother as she does."

"Did you tell her this?" Brian asks.

"I've been telling her for years now. She doesn't

listen. Every time I try to talk about my feelings she tells me to go to church and give up my feelings to God. But God doesn't answer back. And yesterday, she said I'm never going to be a whole person unless I learn how to love Jesus. She said I should just give up if I'm not prepared to sacrifice myself for him."

"She has a point," Brian tells him. "Jesus can help guide the way."

"I don't need saving. I need a parent. I need someone who believes in me. I don't have that right now. I might never have that again."

"You have to believe Jesus will lead the way."

"I've tried that. It doesn't work."

"You're not trying hard enough. You have to really believe, Martin."

Martin starts to cry. The room goes quiet. No one knows what to do.

I've had enough of this. I get up from my seat and put my arm around Martin. I stand him up and walk him back to our room.

"You were brave in there tonight," I tell him.

"Thanks."

"Do you feel any better?"

"I don't feel anything anymore."

Martin sits at the desk by the window.

"Do you want me to get you anything?" I ask.

"I'm fine," he says.

Paul and Randall hang back at the door until I motion them in.

"Is everything okay?" Paul asks when he sees Martin slumped in the chair.

"Martin is feeling emotional," I tell him.

"What else is new?" Randall says.

"Now is not the time, Randall," I say.

"He's never given me a break. I don't know why I should give him one," he says.

"What would Jesus do, Randall?" Paul asks. When Randall doesn't have a smart answer, Paul turns back to Martin. "They're having a sing-along by the campfire. Want to come? It might cheer you up."

"You guys go ahead. I want to be alone," Martin says.

"I'll stay here with you," I say.

"No really. You and Paul should spend some time together," Martin says. "You guys haven't been the same since the fight about Rhonda."

Paul and I look at each other.

"What's that supposed to mean?" Randall asks.

"I think it means Martin wants to be alone," Paul says. "Come on guys. Let's give him his space."

Walking towards the bonfire I tell Paul, "I'm really worried about Martin. I've never seen him this low before."

"He's just trying to get attention," Randall breaks in. "Don't let him ruin your good time."

"You don't understand. He went to a very dark place in Tough Talk tonight. It sounds like things with his grandmother are really bad."

"Indians are never happy unless they're reminding you how bad they have it," Randall says. "You're too nice to him. I'm sure he'll be fine by the time we come back from the bonfire."

I hate to say it, but Randall is right. After a couple

of songs I do start to feel better. Sarah is sitting next to Paul. I watch her as she takes his hand in hers. She looks into his eyes while she sings out of key at the top of her lungs. Every so often Paul looks at me, and smiles. It's nice to see him happy, even if it's not with me. Maybe whatever we had is over. But at least I don't feel like he hates me. Maybe I can live with this, whatever this is.

Martin is still sitting at the desk by the window when the three of us get back to the room. I go to wake him up to go to bed. Something crunches under my shoe as I get close. Several insulin cartridges are on the floor.

"Martin?" I say, pushing his shoulder. "Martin wake up!"

Paul comes over and shakes Martin by the shoulders. But he's not responding.

"Randall! Go get Brian!" Paul says.

"What's going on now?" Randall asks in a huff.

"Just do as I say," Paul yells at him. "Adam, help me get him on the floor. I'm going to give him CPR."

I scoop Martin under his armpits and Paul takes him by the ankles. We lower him to the floor. Paul starts pressing on Martin's chest with both hands. I feel like I'm going to faint. But I have to keep it together. The last thing Paul needs right now is two unconscious roommates to revive.

19 Thoughts and Prayers

BRIAN HOLDS MY HAND and Paul's. We are waiting in the hall outside the phone room while Randall speaks to his parents. Brian's hand feels soft in mine, like one of those spongy stress balls. If I'm squeezing too hard, he doesn't let on.

Paul, Randall, and I slept on cots in the media room last night. When we woke up this morning, Bishop gave us the option of going home. He wants us to call our parents to discuss it first.

"How are you guys holding up?" Brian asks.

My knees won't stop shaking. "I think I'm still in shock," I say.

Paul just looks like he'd fall down if Brian let go of his hand. "After you're done here you should both pray to calm your nerves," Brian tells us.

The door opens and Randall emerges, smiling. "That was exactly what I needed," Randall says. "Mom can talk me down from any ledge."

"Have you decided to stay or go?" Brian asks him.

"Stay of course! I feel bad for Martin, but it's not like we were friends."

"I'm glad you've decided to stay," Brian says. "But you might want to pray on your feelings for Martin. He needs our thoughts and prayers right now."

"Oh for sure," Randall says. "Is the mess hall still open for breakfast?"

"It should be."

"I'll catch up with guys in a bit," Randall leaves the three of us in the hall.

"Who's next?" Brian says.

"Do you mind if I go next?" I say to Paul. "I want to get this over with. I'll try not to be too long."

"Go ahead," Paul says.

I take a seat in front of the rotary phone. My hands shake as I lift up the receiver and dial the number. Mom picks up after a couple of rings.

"Mom? It's me Adam."

"Adam! What a surprise! How is camp?"

I start crying into her ear.

"Adam, what's wrong?" She sounds concerned.

"One of my roommates tried to kill himself last night by shooting himself up with insulin."

"That's awful! That poor soul. Is he going to live?"

"Bishop spoke with the doctor this morning. He'll pull through. We found him just in time."

"Jesus sent you to find him before he did something he would regret for all eternity."

"I beg your pardon?"

"You don't need me to tell you suicide is a one-way ticket to hell, Adam."

"My friend tried to kill himself and all you care about is if he's going to hell?"

"It doesn't matter the cross you have to bear, Adam. Suicide is a sin."

"Mom, you're supposed to be comforting me, not judging my friend."

"I'm doing the best I can."

I pull the receiver away from my ear and look at it. It's like I'm speaking to my mother for the very first time. She's a complete stranger to me. A stranger I don't like much.

"Adam? Are you there?" Her voice sounds fake and tinny coming out of the receiver.

I put the phone back to my ear "Mom, what would you do if I killed myself?"

"Are you considering killing yourself?"

"It's just a question."

"I can't talk to you when you're in this state."

"Mom, I really need to know who you care about more: Jesus or me?"

There is silence on the line. I just got my answer.

"I need to go," I say. "My roommate is waiting for the phone."

"I'll keep your friend in my prayers."

"You do that." When I hang up the phone it feels like a door has closed.

Brian smiles when he sees me come out of the office. "How did it go?" he asks me.

"Pretty much how I expected."

"Are you going to stay or go home?" Paul asks me.

"You know, I completely forgot to talk about it with my mother," I say.

"That's okay. You don't have to decide right this minute. Take your time," Brian says.

"Thanks. I'm feeling a little dizzy. Do you mind if I go lie down for a bit?" I ask.

"Sure thing. I'll be by to check on you in a bit."

"Thanks, Brian."

I use the walls to help me keep my balance. I forget where I'm going and end up back at room 120 instead of the media room where they moved us. Martin's things are already gone. It's like he was never here. It's like when Rhonda ran away from the camp and Bishop asked us all to pretend we couldn't see her. It's like pretending your problems never happened will make them all go away.

I go back to the media room to grab my sketchbook. Outside are small prayer circles of campers scattered across the lawn, praying for Martin's soul. I hide behind some boulders on a small ledge that looks out over the side of the mountain. I spend the next fifteen minutes trying to sketch Martin's face. But my memory of him is already fading. I put my book down and clasp my hands to pray.

"Dear God, please show me the path towards peace so that I may learn to love with all my heart and live my life to its fullest."

"Adam?"

I look up and behind me. The sun is directly behind Paul, forming a halo around his head.

"How did you find me?" I ask.

"Rhonda saw you walking this way. Do you mind if I sit with you?"

"Please do."

Paul sits right up close to me. He takes my hand and holds it between both of his. "I'm sorry for how I behaved this week."

"No, I'm sorry. It wasn't fair of me to force my beliefs on you."

"The thing is, I think what you did was amazing. It took a lot of guts for you defend Rhonda the way you did. I wish I was that brave."

"I'm not brave, believe me. I still can't decide if I should stay or go home, even though the choice is pretty clear."

"I wish you would stay here with me, even if it's only for one more week. You're the first person I've met that I want to be with. I'm worried that if I don't explore these feelings now I never will."

"That's not true."

"Yes it is. If I keep hiding my feelings, I'm going to end up hating myself. What if the pain gets to be so great I try to make it stop like Martin did?"

"Promise me you'll never do that." I kiss Paul's

hands. "Promise me you'll never hurt yourself."

Paul pulls me to him and we hug so hard I never want to let go. I feel like a whole person in his arms, like the person I was meant to be. We stop hugging for a moment and look into each other's eyes. Without thinking, I lean in and kiss him softly on the lips. I pull away to see his reaction. He smiles and leans over. We kiss again. It's my first real kiss and my head is swirling with confusion, grief, and love.

"Adam?"

I stop kissing Paul long enough to see Randall standing on the path, his mouth open. Then he runs back towards the lodge.

"We have to stop him before he tells Bishop," Paul says.

"Wait." I hold Paul back by the arm. "It's time Randall and I had a long talk."

20 True Colours

RANDALL IS RUNNING FAST towards the lodge. I try to chase him without causing a scene in front of the other campers.

"Randall, wait!" I shout. Randall doesn't even look back. "Can we just go somewhere and talk?"

Randall stops in his tracks. He tilts his head to catch some air, and then bends over with his hands on his hips. I can't tell if he's stopping because I got through to him or if he's in worse shape than I am.

"Thanks for stopping," I tell him when I catch up.

"You have ten minutes," Randall says between pants.

Randall takes me back to room 120. He checks the other rooms in the hall to make sure that no one is around. He peeks into Brian's room to make sure he's not there.

"No one will bother us here," Randall says, once we're inside. "Everyone is avoiding this place. This hall oozes evil."

I go behind the bunk that we shared so no one will able to see us.

"Why did you tell Bishop about my crush on Paul?" I ask him.

"What are you talking about?" Randall tries to look puzzled.

"Your eyes are betraying your mouth," I tell him. "Look me in the eye and tell me you didn't tell Bishop I had a crush on Paul."

Randall looks me square in the eye. He's about to open his mouth to speak. But he chickens out and looks away. "I know you don't like me, Adam. You have no idea how much that hurts me. I saw you first, and I knew we should be close. But then Paul seemed to take up all your attention. It's like the rest of the world disappears whenever he's around. I really wanted you for me."

"If the reason you told on me was to make me like you, it didn't work."

"No, but it gave you a taste of how lousy I felt being around you two. Did you ever once think about how I feel? Did it occur to you that I was being mean because I was dying on the inside?"

I feel kind of sorry for Randall. I always suspected he had a crush on me, but it was more annoying than flattering. If Paul had developed a crush on Randall or Martin instead of me, I would probably be eating my heart out too.

"I'm sorry," I tell him. "I didn't mean to hurt you. I'd never had a crush on a boy before. I kind of lost my head."

"All I wanted was for you to like me as much as you like Paul," Randall starts to cry.

Randall struck me as the type of person who hides his emotions behind perfection. I'm not even sure how to comfort him. I put my hand on his shoulder to show support. But then he pulls me in for a hug, almost knocking the air out of me. I hug him back for a bit. Then I let my arms fall to my sides, signalling the hug to be over. But Randall doesn't get the signal. He presses his crotch against mine and starts licking my neck. I try to push Randall away, but he's too strong. He tries to kiss me on the mouth.

"Stop it," I push him away so hard he nearly falls over. "What is wrong with you?"

"What do you see in that guy? He's doesn't even want to be gay. I could give you everything you want! We could be perfect Christians in public and have sex behind closed doors! No one would suspect a thing."

"I'm not looking to have sex. Especially not secret sex. I want to feel a connection with someone."

"But Paul is *Asian*!"

"You know, Randall, I actually felt sorry for you for a couple of minutes. But then I remembered the reason I care about Paul is he's everything you're not. You're just going through the motions of being Christian. Hell, you're probably just going through the motions of being gay. Paul might be confused, but at least he's exploring his emotions."

"I should go to Bishop right now and tell him I caught you two kissing."

"Then I'll tell him you forced yourself on me."

"Who do you think Bishop is going to believe? Me or you?" Randall crosses his arms in front of his chest. He's right. He has all the power.

I realize that this is the third time this summer someone has wielded their power over me. First it was Greta, then my parents, and now Randall. I'm tired of it.

"You know what?" I say. "I'll tell Bishop the whole thing. Right before I leave the camp."

"What?"

"You heard me. I wasn't sure if I should stay or go home. But you helped me make up my mind. You won. Are you happy now?"

"I don't believe you. You're just bluffing so I won't tell."

"Come with me to see Bishop if you want. Just leave Paul out of it. Paul needs this place more than I do. Let him have that."

Randall looks confused. He obviously can't tell if he's won or lost the battle. As for me, I feel more focused than I've ever been in my life.

21 One Door Closes

PAUL WATCHES ME as I shove my clothes into my backpack. Randall was supposed to supervise my packing, but he stormed out of our room when he saw Paul was already there. I'm still angry at Randall, but I'm trying to stay calm. I don't know if this is the last time I'll see Paul again.

"Did you tell Bishop that we kissed?" Paul asks me.

"No. As far as Bishop is concerned, my feelings for you are one-sided."

"Then I don't see why you have to go home now. Why not just spend one more night to say goodbye to your friends?"

"Bishop thinks it's better that I go home sooner than later. He said it's like ripping a Band-Aid off a cut."

That's only half true. Bishop doesn't want me to spend another night at the lodge, because he's worried I'll turn Paul into a "full-fledged gay."

"You're not mad that I decided to stay?" Paul asks.

"Of course not. Are you mad at me for wanting to leave?"

"I'm not mad. But it does sort of feel like you're abandoning me."

"I'm not abandoning you. I asked God for a sign and he sent you to come find me," I try to explain. "This place isn't for me. This *religion* isn't for me. It's all so black and white. It's like being a good person means nothing if you're gay, or if you have sex before marriage."

"But you just said that you asked God for a sign," Paul says. "And you got it."

"God's not the one I'm having a problem with. It's the people who claim to be his followers." I shove the last of my clothes into my bag. "If Camp Revelation has taught me anything, it's that I can be spiritual without being religious."

"I wish we hadn't kissed," Paul admits.

"What do you mean?"

"It happened so soon after Martin tried to kill himself. I'm still not sure if I was kissing you because I like you or because I was sad." He puts his hands on his head like he has headache.

There's a knock on the door and Brian pokes his head into the room. He sees the look of pain on Paul's face. "Is everything okay? I thought Randall was supposed to be here making sure Adam gets ready to go."

"He's off praying somewhere," I say.

"Are you ready?" Brian asks.

"I just zipped up my bag."

"I guess this is goodbye," Paul says. He holds out his hand for me to shake. "It was nice meeting you."

"It was nice meeting you too," I tell him. I take his hand in mine. There's no secret handshake this time. We shake hands the way you do in a job interview.

I follow Brian to the common area where Brad is running a Bible Study. Brad stops talking and everyone looks at me. Then they look away. I wouldn't be surprised if Bishop arranged this with Brad to remind me I had been kicked out of the flock. It works. I feel lonely and scared. But if I have to turn into Randall to be the Christian my parents want me to be, then I don't belong in this flock.

Brian jingles his keys as we walk towards his car.

"Wait up! Wait up!"

Brian and I turn around to see Rhonda running with her luggage to catch up with us.

"What do you want?" Brian asks her.

"I'm going home too," she says. "As soon as Randall told me Bishop was letting you go home, I banged on his door until he let me go too."

"See the fire you started?" Brian says to me.

"I didn't start the fire," I say. "It was already burning when I got here."

Rhonda and I get in the back of Brian's car. Rhonda rests her head on my shoulder as we start the long drive back to Squamish. Three hours later, we're back in the parking lot of the Walmart where the bus picked us up. Brian hands us the plastic bags with our cell phones.

"Oh wait, I almost forgot this," Brian hands me my *Archie Digest*.

"I completely forgot about this," I tell him.

"I hope you don't mind that I read it."

"Not at all. I hope you enjoyed it."

"I did actually," Brian says. "I'll pray for you both."

Three quick car honks sound not far from where we're standing.

"There's my aunt!" Rhonda says. She hugs me and gives me a peck on the cheek. "I'll add you to Snapchat as soon as I get in the car! Promise you'll accept."

"I promise."

Rhonda runs in the direction of her aunt's car.

"Do you want me to wait until your family gets here?" Brian asks me as we watch Rhonda and her aunt drive away.

"I'll be fine now that I have my phone."

"Are you sure? I feel weird just dumping you here."

"It's for the better."

"Here's my number in case something goes wrong. I don't mind coming back to get you."

"I'll be fine."

Brian gets back in his car and drives off.

I stand by myself in the parking lot. I turn on my phone for the first time in weeks. Sure enough, Rhonda's friend request is waiting for me on Snapchat.

A car horn is honked to get my attention. Mike gets out of the front passenger seat.

"It's so good to see you," Mike says, hugging me.

"You too!"

"Mom, this is Adam," he says over his shoulder.

"So nice to meet you, Adam," she says, waving from behind the steering wheel.

"Thanks for putting me up while I figure out what I'm going to do next," I tell her.

"I'm glad to help. Let me pop the trunk open for you."

I throw my duffel back into the trunk. I look up at the mountains I just came from and wonder if Paul is looking down at me.

"Hurry up," Mike shouts from his window. "I want to get the hell out of here before someone catches us at Walmart."

22 Melriches

MIKE AND I ARE STANDING outside of Melriches coffee shop on Davie Street. The start of fall is still a few days away, but it already feels like sweater weather.

"Are you sure you don't want me to keep you company until he gets here?" Mike asks.

"I'll be fine. I need some time alone to prepare myself."

"All right. I'll pretend to go shopping for clothes I can't afford. Call me when you're done."

"Will do."

Mike hugs me before he crosses the street.

I treat myself to a London Fog and find a seat facing the door. I look at the vintage kitchen clock on the wall. I'm ten minutes early. I pull my sketchbook out of my backpack and start to draw the Goth barista as a superhero.

I look up every time I hear the door open. The sun is shining through the glass, turning everyone's face into a black blob as they enter the shop. The faces don't come into focus until the bodies take their place in line.

Someone taps me on the shoulder from behind, and I whirl around in my seat. Paul's face is smiling down at me. I stand up and nearly break his nose with the top of my head.

"I'm sorry! You surprised me. It didn't occur to me you would come in through the back door."

"I'm fine, you didn't get me," he says. "I didn't mean to startle you. I found a parking spot in the back. Let me grab a drink."

I can't help but notice that he didn't try to hug me. Did Bishop do a number on him after I left Camp Revelation?

"It's so good to see you," he says, sitting down across from me. "I'm sorry I waited so long to connect with you. A lot has been going on."

"I understand. My life went completely upside down after I left the camp. Things are only beginning to feel normal again."

"How have you been? What's been going on?"

"I'm living with a friend and his parents. They've been great. I told them about what happened to Martin and they set me up with a counsellor. That's been really helpful. It feels strange not to be living at home. But Mike and his parents are exactly what I need right now."

"Do you talk to your parents?"

"Here and there. Mom is ready to start listening. The last time we spoke she said she was open to the idea of non-Christian family counselling."

"It's as good a start as any," Paul says, nodding.

"My dad still doesn't want anything to do with me. And that's fine. I don't want anything to do with him right now either."

"Harsh," Paul says.

"Was that a really mean thing to say?" I ask.

"I just can't imagine being that angry at my dad."

"You don't have my dad."

"I guess not." Paul looks into his hot chocolate. "Do you talk to Rhonda?"

"All the time. She's living with her aunt. She says Hi, by the way. You should friend her on social media."

"I've been meaning to," Paul says. "Were you able to get hold of Martin?"

"No. I Googled him but nothing came up."

"Same here. I hope he's okay."

"So do I."

We both stare into our drinks. I'm tempted to pull out my phone and look at it for no reason.

"I told my parents about you," Paul says.

"You did?"

"I didn't want to hide what happened from them in case they found out from someone."

"What exactly did you tell them?"

"The truth. That we met and that I like you as more than a friend. And that when you left the lodge it felt like the whole world had been pulled out from under me."

"What did they say?"

"That they loved me."

"Wow. That is the complete opposite of what happened when I told my parents."

"I know. I almost feel guilty telling you. But things *have* changed between my parents and me."

"I'm sorry I sent all those messages. I felt like things weren't finished between us when I left."

"It's okay. I wanted to respond right away, but my parents asked that I wait and pray first. It was good advice."

"I understand if this is goodbye. If you want to go our separate ways." Saying it feels like the hardest thing I've had to do. But it has to be his decision. "My life is completely screwed right now. The last thing I want is to drag you into my drama."

"Your drama is my drama," Paul says firmly. "You are the only other gay Christian I know who understands what I'm going through."

"I never thought of it that way. So we can be friends."

"Can we be friends that hold hands?"

"That depends. Can you hold hands with someone who's losing his religion?"

"Only if you can hold hands with someone who's clinging to his religion for answers."

Paul puts his hand on mine. Then he leans over the table and kisses me on the forehead.

"Why are you crying?" Paul says, noticing the tears on my face. "Everything has worked out!"

"It's Martin," I say, my voice breaking. "It feels wrong to feel so happy after what happened to him. I keep thinking I could have helped him more."

"I know. I blame myself for not seeing it coming," Paul squeezes my hand.

"I said the same thing to my counsellor."

"What did he say?"

"He said that I'm not helping Martin by feeling sorry for myself. He thinks the best way to honour Martin's life is to live as openly and honestly as I can."

"Then that's what we'll do." Paul holds up his hand. "Secret handshake?"

"Secret handshake," I say.

We lock thumbs and flutter our fingers like wings, up, up until our hands can't reach anymore. For the first time in a long time, it feels like everything is going to be okay.

Acknowledgements

I could not have asked for a better editor than Kat Mototsune for guiding this book from concept to completion. Thanks Kat for listening to my mid-morning ramblings as I talked through the characters and plot, as well as your comments and insights on spirituality and the true meaning of love.

I would not have had the courage to write this book were it not for the love and support of Mette Bach and Billeh Nickerson. You are both an inspiration to me.

Lastly, to my peeps who put up with me while I wrote this book: Dean Mirau, Ryan Wylie, Dan Harwood, Chris Dorey, and Bren Robbins. They say no man is a failure who has friends; I am living proof of that.